The Greatest Idea Ever

The Greatest Idea Ever

by Joan Carris

illustrated by Carol Newsom

J. B. Lippincott  New York

Library of Congress Cataloging-in-Publication Data
Carris, Joan Davenport.
   The greatest idea ever / Joan Carris.
      p.   cm.
   Summary: Fourth grade is a time of turmoil for the irrepressible
Gus, whose imaginative ideas constantly get him into trouble as he
tries to train his new dog, organizes a school art show, and battles
his enemy Nanny Vincent.
   ISBN 0-397-32378-6. — ISBN 0-397-32379-4 (lib. bdg.)
   [.1 Schools—Fiction.   2. Dogs—Fiction.   3. Artists—Fiction.]
I. Title.
PZ7.C2347Gr 1990   89-34516
[Fic]—dc20   CIP
                                                                AC

For Brad,
the source of so many great ideas

CONTENTS

1

The Trouble with Winter

"Barfo!" Gus looked at the gray January skies and the tired little piles of snow beside the curb.

"Barfo!" he said again, just in case the world had not heard him the first time. He shifted the backpack on his shoulders and kept on walking to school.

School wasn't the problem. Gus's fourth-grade class had a new young teacher, Mr. Keene. "He's cool," Gus had told his parents way back in September. "He plays the guitar and knows all kinds of great songs. He divides us into teams for math contests and spelling bees. And he

1

doesn't go all red and holler if somebody just throws a spitball."

Now, late in January, school was still okay. Then why did he feel so grumpy? Was it January? Nobody liked winter in southern Ohio very much. It was too cold for sports and there was rarely enough snow to play in.

"Hey, Gus! Wait up!" Pepper Browning tore across his front yard. He hopped over the hedge and joined Gus on the sidewalk. "Hey!" he said again, doing a couple of fast knee bends. Pepper was serious about exercise. "I have to get in shape for spring soccer," he kept saying. Pepper ran everywhere.

"Yo," Gus said in greeting. "What're we doing today after school?"

"I don't know." Pep shrugged his shoulders.

Gus sighed. That must be the problem. Nothing to do. Last fall he'd gone fishing with his brothers and they had explored the cave east of town. That had been fun.

After smashing times in England, he hadn't been at all sure that he wanted to return to America. Gus's family had spent nearly three years in England because of his father's growing computer business. Back home in Hampshire, Gus's greatest worry had been how to make new friends.

But Buzzer and Pep were in his class, and they were great. Then Thanksgiving had come, with his oldest brother Jut home from college, and Christmas.

And now dead old winter.

"It's so boring," Gus said.

"Sure is," Pep agreed, catching his mood. "Maybe Buzzer'll think of something."

Gus shook his head. "He never has any good ideas."

"You do. You get great ideas! Remember the day we hid Keene's grade book and he went crazy looking for it, and all the time it was taped under his own chair?" Pepper chortled at the memory.

"And the time we tied the handle on the john door so those dumb girls couldn't get out?" added Gus.

"Hee, hee," Pepper laughed again. "That was terrific!"

"Too bad the principal didn't think so," Gus replied. But he was thinking, I do get great ideas. I just haven't been working at it lately.

Gus hopped up the front steps of the school. He felt fine now. He just needed an idea— something to do with all the wonderful time after school.

"Yo, Buzz!" he called across the classroom. Buzzer was really Roger Thane. When his two-year-old sister had first seen him in the hospital's nursery window, she had called her brother "my buzzer." She had called him Buzzer so long it had stuck.

"Yo-oh!" Buzzer hollered back across the room.

"Hey, guys, can it," Mr. Keene said. "Save the wagon train yells for recess, okay? Everybody sit down so we can get started."

Gus opened his spelling workbook and began to draw in the margins. He always drew when he was thinking. What can we do after school that's different? he asked himself as he drew Mr. Keene.

4

In the workbook Mr. Keene's blond, curly hair spilled down onto his shoulders. He had legs like a stork and more curly hair on his chest. The chest hair showed right through his shirt. His hands were jammed into his pockets. Gus wasn't very good at drawing hands. A line went from Mr. Keene's mouth to a balloon above his head. Gus was deciding what to write in the little balloon when he felt a hand on his shoulder.

"Do I really look like that?" Mr. Keene asked.

Gus looked up. "No, this is a cartoon. But I think I made the hair too long."

"A trifle," Mr. Keene said dryly. "Let's do spelling now, okay? Save the cartoons for some other time."

At lunch, Gus said to Pep and Buzzer, "Still no idea. Sorry. Any other day, I'd have had forty great ideas by now!"

"It's okay," began Buzzer, changing abruptly to a whisper. "Hey, look, you guys. Nanny Vincent and her friends are coming to our table."

5

"She wouldn't dare." Pep made a face at the advancing group of girls. "They haven't talked to us since we locked 'em in the john."

"There's nowhere else to sit," Gus observed, scanning the crowded lunchroom. "Anyway it's okay. I got an idea."

Nanny Vincent and her friends Bethie and Tina sat as far away from the boys as the table would allow. They talked to each other and ate their spaghetti and acted as if they were in another county.

Gus liked everyone in his class except Nanny Vincent. Her light-colored eyes were always busy watching for a boy to break a rule so that she could report him. She had pale hair and pale skin to match her eyes. All autumn she had made fun of his English accent and the words he used—something he couldn't help after so much time in an English school.

What Gus hated most was Nanny's tattling. She'd been telling on him all year. Even way back in kindergarten she had been bossy, he thought, before he'd moved away.

Gus glanced down the table at Nanny, who sat on his side of the bench. Yes, his idea would work.

"Hey, Nanny," Gus called.

Nanny twitched her head as if to shake off a pesky fly.

"What're you doing?" Pep asked Gus.

Gus shook his head warningly at Pep and Buzzer.

"Hey, Nanny, isn't that your mom out in the hall?" Gus pointed to the windowed hall door. "She just went by."

Nanny gave him a glance that would have frozen molten lava. But slowly she stood up and leaned toward the door to peer out the window. Her friends turned to look out, too.

Instantly Gus slid down the bench and set her plate of spaghetti on the seat behind her. He scooted back to his own end before Nanny or her friends turned around.

Buzzer and Pep grinned at him and waited.

"Just bug off, Gus," Nanny said frostily. "*I* don't see her. Anyway if she was here she'd know we were all having lunch." She wrinkled her nose at him and sat down with an angry flounce.

Buzzer and Pep leaned forward, howling with laughter. Nanny gave a frantic glance at the table where her spaghetti ought to have been.

"Sssh!" Gus hissed at Pep and Buzzer. "Nobody saw me do it! Just act cool."

"Ooooh!" Nanny wailed as she stood up. The plate stuck briefly to her pants before it clattered onto the bench and then to the floor. The spaghetti stayed on Nanny.

"Gus Howard!" she screeched. Her face turned a livid purple as she strained to look at the mess on her clothes.

She gets a real interesting color when she's mad, Gus thought. He saw the lunchroom aide hurrying to their table. Within a few minutes, Gus was standing in front of the principal's desk.

"We meet again," Mr. Rawson said without humor. He was a short, round man who stared right into a student's eyes.

Gus nodded. "I, uh . . . I should have thought about it more, Mr. Rawson. I apologize."

"I see. And if you had thought more about it, what would you have done?"

Gus smiled. "I wouldn't have gotten caught."

Mr. Rawson's eyebrows shot upward. "You mean you'd do it again if you were sure not to be caught?"

"Probably," Gus admitted. "I mean, yes, sir. I hate Nanny Vincent."

This time Mr. Rawson's eyebrows met in the middle of his forehead in a frown. "Gus, you know we can't allow this behavior in school. Your parents are not going to be happy to hear from me again."

"I know. Maybe, this time, we could just not tell them? Then they won't be so unhappy."

The principal shook his head. "Gus, I'd like to find out why you're getting in trouble. If Mr. Keene weren't your teacher, I think you'd be in here about once a week. Now why is that? Aren't you happy to be back home in Hampshire?"

Gus shifted from one foot to the other. "Well, sort of, but I had tons of friends in England, and lots to do all the time. Like conker fights—conkers are the same as buckeyes—and polo matches. Polo's really fun, and they have smashing teas in the clubhouse—"

"Not in *January*," Mr. Rawson interrupted. "However, I catch your meaning. Moving is rough. But Mr. Keene tells me you have two good friends, Buzzer Thane and Pepper Browning. And you'll make more friends. Hating your classmates—little Nanny Vincent for instance—is not the answer, Gus."

"She's a tattletale and a weasel and—"

"Stop right there, my friend. If you cannot get along with her, then keep away from her. This is my final warning. Next time you'll stay after school. Is that clear?"

"Yes, sir. Can I go now, sir?"

Gus took his time returning to the fourth-grade classroom. He stopped off at the water fountain, remembering with glee how furious Nanny had been. It had been worth apologizing to her in front of their lunch table. He knew *she* knew that he wasn't one bit sorry.

He slipped into his seat as the class started social studies. In his workbook, Gus began to draw again. He needed a good idea before the bell rang at three fifteen.

2

Gone to the Dogs

Mr. Keene looked down at Gus's social studies workbook. "Who is it this time?" he asked, peering at the colored-pencil art.

"It's Pepper," Gus answered.

The drawing showed Pep's gloriously wild head of red hair and his off-center, appealing grin. He was running, of course, and the picture caught the free, pumping movements of his legs and arms.

"Dumb of me to ask," Mr. Keene said, studying the picture. "It's obviously Pepper Browning." He squatted next to Gus's desk. "However," he whispered into Gus's ear, "we're supposed to be writing about Africa. You're going to art in a few minutes. There you can draw the rest of the afternoon. Deal?" He stood up and held out his hand.

Gus shook hands. "Sorry. I need an idea, and I always draw when I'm thinking. I guess it's a bad habit."

Mr. Keene managed to smile and look serious at the same time. "Your drawing is too good to be a bad habit, Gus. I'll give you an idea if you want one. Artists like you should be taking classes at the art museum."

"Artists are wimps," Gus said.

"Only a troglodyte would make a remark like that," Mr. Keene said loftily, moving down the aisle.

"What's a troglodyte?" Gus called after him.

"Look it up. Mr. Webster knows. It begins t-r-o-g-l-o-." He sat down at his desk.

Nanny Vincent shot out of her seat and marched toward the big Webster's dictionary atop the bookcase by the window. Gus was right behind her. He was going to punch her out if she didn't let him have it first. Nobody had told *her* to look anything up!

"Please take your seat, Nanny," Mr. Keene said.

"I got here first," she insisted.

"Sit down, Nanny, until Gus is finished," the teacher said. "Everyone else get back to work."

Nanny stomped to her seat as Gus turned to the "T" section in the dictionary. He found "troglodyte" and read the entry. Smiling, he returned to his seat.

"Well?" asked Mr. Keene. "Tell the class what a troglodyte is, Gus."

"A dodo," Gus said, still smiling. "An ig-no-ra-mus," he added, emphasizing each syllable.

"Right. Anyone who thinks that artists are wimps is not very intelligent. Remember Michelangelo, who painted beautiful pictures on the ceiling of the Sistine Chapel in Italy? That's darn hard work.

"And this is enough of a break. Everyone get back to your papers on Africa, and I mean right now."

Finally, in art class, Gus had an idea. It wasn't fantastic, but it was the best he could do.

He was drawing when the idea came to him. He had drawn Buzzer at his desk—his white-blond head bent over his paper on Africa, his short legs tucked under the desk. Then he added Grace to the drawing. She was Buzzer's collie dog. She looked just right in the picture, sitting next to the desk, her leash in her mouth, waiting for Buzzer to finish.

Grace was a terrific dog. Just looking at her gold-and-white furry body in the drawing made Gus want to pet her.

That was when the idea came. At the Hampshire pound were lots of dogs that needed petting. Gus's older brother Marty, now a high school senior, had spent many volunteer hours there. He had groomed, walked, and fed all their dogs.

Why not us? Gus thought. Why not me and Buzzer and Pep? At least it would be something different. He remembered his family's old basset hound, Pierpont, dead now for several years. His hair had been short and stiff—wrong for petting. And he had always smelled like a hound. Grace smelled good. And she was nice and furry.

"Go where?" asked Pep after school. He was trotting backward down the sidewalk, ahead of Gus and Buzzer.

"The dog pound," Gus repeated. "We can brush the dogs or maybe just play with them. They'll love it!"

"Yeah," Buzzer said, "but some of those dogs bite. That's why they're there. They're gonna die, you know, if nobody adopts them."

"If we brush them and make them look better, maybe somebody'll give them homes!" Gus protested. "You got a better idea?"

Buzzer shrugged. "I think my mom'll say no."

"Then don't . . . tell her," Pepper said, beginning to puff slightly. "We'll say we're going . . . on our bikes. I need roadwork . . . anyway." Since he had begun training for soccer season, he called all bike riding roadwork.

"Great idea," said Gus, "except I might have trouble getting out of the house if Mr. Rawson's called Mom. She's friends with Nanny's mother. Isn't that gross?"

"Gross," Pepper agreed. "Look . . . I'll be at Buzzer's. Call us . . . there," he said as he back-pedaled down the sidewalk to his hedge. He tried hopping backward over the hedge and fell in a heap on his backpack.

"I'll be there in a few minutes, Buzz!" Pepper yelled as he lay on his back.

Buzzer turned right onto Willow, just a block before Gus's house on the corner of Hillside and Grove.

When Gus stepped into the kitchen, his mother was there waiting for him. "Sit down. I want to talk to you."

Gus threw back the hood of his parka and slumped into a chair at the table. "Mr. Rawson called, hunh?"

"He did. Gus, I need to understand why you are picking on Nanny Vincent. First you trapped her in the john and now this spaghetti business. And Mr. Rawson says there have been other, minor incidents. I don't get it. You've always been nice to people."

"Look, Mom, Nanny hates my guts. All last fall she made fun of my accent and the words I used. Nobody else cared if I forgot and said *loo* for bathroom or *lorry* for truck, but she made a big hairy deal out of it! She's always ordering me around, and she tells on people. She *loves* to tell on people! Especially *me*!"

Gus's mom leaned her chin in her hands and thought.

"I hate tattling," she said after a bit. "I'm sure that Mrs. Vincent wouldn't want her daughter to be a telltale. But Nanny's just being temporarily difficult, Gus, and I want you to leave her politely alone. We live in a small town. We have to be as nice to one another as possible."

"Come on, Mom! I have to be nice to Nanny when she's being rotten to me?"

"It's the only way she'll ever learn. The more you pick on her, the worse she'll get. It's called a vicious circle."

"Why can't she be nice *first*? Then I'll be nice back."

His mom smiled and reached over to ruffle his hair. "Because you can do it better. You're one of the nicest people I know. The others are Dad, Jut, Marty, and Nick."

"Oh, poop." Gus looked down at the table. When he looked up, she was still smiling at him. "I didn't promise yet, did I?"

"No, but you're going to if you want to live to grow up." She chuckled.

"It isn't worth it."

"Yes it is. Being grown up is absolutely wonderful. Now I want to hear your promise."

"Okay—but I'm going to be sorry I promised. I just know it!"

"Maybe not. Ask Buzzer and Pep to help you keep your promise. They're nice guys. They'll understand."

"*Never,*" said Gus, dying to change the subject. "Mom, can I go bike riding with them now? We're sick of being inside all the time."

Gus's mom said yes, and by four o'clock he, Pep, and Buzzer were standing at the ancient wooden desk that nearly filled the small office of the Hampshire Pound.

"Pet the dogs?" old Mrs. Long said vaguely. "Groom them?" She leaned over the desk to examine the three boys. "You children don't look very old to me. Do your parents know you're here?"

Gus spoke quickly. "We sort of got this job from my brother, Marty Howard. He came here all through junior high, before we moved to England. He took care of lots of your dogs, Mrs. Long. Remember?"

The elderly lady brightened. "Marty? Yes, of course. A wonderful boy. All our animals loved him. Where did you say he is now?"

"He's here, in high school, but he's too busy so he sent us." Gus felt guilty, but only for a second. Marty would have sent them if he had known they wanted to come.

"Just tell the kennel man then," Mrs. Long said, pointing to a door. "Go through there and tell Walter you're Marty's brother. He's sure to remember."

The moment the door creaked open, every dog in the long cinderblock building burst into howls.

"Geez!" Buzzer yelped. "Are you sure we wanta do this?" He put his hands over his ears.

A square man in coveralls hurried toward them, shushing dogs as he came. "Hello, boys. What can we do for you? How about a nice beagle puppy? I've got four back here that are purebreds for sure."

Gus explained about his brother Marty and they all introduced themselves.

"What about a nice kitty?" Walter offered. "I've got every kind and color in the book. A kitty's no trouble at all. Marty loved the kittens." He led them down the row, explaining the personalities of each animal.

"Stay away from that fellow. See the sign on his cage? He's a biter. I sure hope some farmer wants a watchdog."

"I told you," Buzzer said.

"Look at this puppy," Pep called out. "Hey, guy, wanta lick my hand?" Pep stuck one hand into the cage.

"Oh, wow," breathed Gus. Here was the puppy of his dreams—an incredibly fuzzy, furry dog that would be wonderful to pet. The puppy's big black eyes gazed into Gus's brown ones as the dog gnawed happily on Pep's hand. When

Gus buried both hands in his fur, the puppy whimpered and wriggled with pleasure.

"What kind of dog is this?" Gus asked.

Walter grinned. "Pure U.S. dog. I'd guess part poodle and part sheepdog. Look at the size of those paws."

Gus held one of the white paws. Both front paws were white and the back paws were black. One eye patch was white, the other black. He was carefully designed all over.

"Can I take him out and brush him?" Gus asked. "We can brush all the dogs—or take them for walks."

Walter moved toward the tackle room. "Got several brushes right here. We'll let the puppies out first. Later, you can take some of the bigger, friendlier dogs into the outside runs. Doesn't anybody want to pet a kitty?"

"I do," Buzzer said. "I've got a dog at home. Mom says we don't need anything else, but I like kittens."

Buzzer spent the next hour up to his chin in kittens. Gus and Pep groomed the dogs. Just before they left, Walter showed them how to

feed the puppies. When chow time was over, the puppies went back to their cages. All but one.

Gus stood outside the fuzzy puppy's cage. He just could not stick this dog back into that little space. This dog was meant to run. He had spent the last hour racing joyously up and down the aisle. Now he was nestled in Gus's arms with his head tucked up under Gus's chin. If I just hold him, Gus thought, he'll go to sleep. He feels safe with me. Happy.

"Hurry up," Pep called. "I have to take out the wastebaskets before supper or I'm burned. Mom'll ground me."

"And I have to walk Grace," Buzzer said.

That did it. The Howards should have a dog, too. They would have gotten one in England, but the landlord of their rented house had said three cats were enough pets.

Gus looked up to find Walter standing beside him. "You like that puppy, don't you?" Walter asked.

"Can I take him home?"

*　*　*　*

Gus pushed his bike home with one hand and held the puppy inside his parka with the other hand. Pep peeled off at his driveway, and later, Buzzer. "Hope your folks like the puppy," Buzzer called back.

3

Just a Figment

"If I don't hear from Iowa State pretty soon, I'm going to explode," Marty was saying as Gus sidled into the kitchen.

Gus was overjoyed to see Marty, who would help to argue for the puppy. Gus pushed the black-and-white head down inside his parka and tried to fade into the wallpaper.

"Just chill out," Nick told Marty. "With your grades, you've got it made." Lately, Nick or someone in the family was always telling Marty to relax. Marty talked of nothing but getting into a college with a good veterinary medicine school. His first choice was Iowa State University.

Nick turned to Gus. "Hey, short stuff, where you been?"

Gus made a face at Nick, who was fourteen and in high school now and very superior.

Nick stared at Gus's lumpy, wiggling parka. "What did you do, swallow a kindergartner?"

"Oh, hi, Gus," his dad said, looking up from the evening paper. He leaned forward slightly, eyeing the parka just like Nick.

Mrs. Howard turned from the sink where she'd been draining the steaming broccoli. She, too, gazed at Gus's bulging coat.

Marty started to chuckle. "I get the first guess. It's live and it eats dog food, right, Gus?"

"Yowp!" said the puppy, thrusting his head out of the parka.

Mr. Howard hid behind his paper. "Tell me that that boy and his dog are figments of my imagination!" he ordered. "I did not see them, especially the dog."

Gus's mom giggled. "Wrong again, Pops," she said as she went toward Gus. "Where did you get him? You aren't planning to keep him, are you?"

Gus didn't say anything. Instead, he unzipped his parka and held up the puppy so everyone could see what a perfect dog he was.

"Geez, he's cute!" said Nick.

"He sure is," Marty said, taking the dog out of Gus's hands and holding him against his chest. "Real soft, too."

"It is not a figment of my imagination," moaned their dad.

Gus had finally thought of the right things to say. "I don't think he'll shed because he's part poodle. And he'll die if we don't give him a home. He came from the pound."

Marty was examining the dog. "Surprise! He is a *she*."

"Oh, dear!" Mrs. Howard closed her eyes.

Marty carried the puppy over to his mother. "Here," he said. "Lick the nice mommy. She likes animals."

Gus beamed. He knew he could count on Marty.

The puppy obligingly licked Mrs. Howard's

cheek, then wiggled to get down. Marty set her on the floor. She ran over to Gus's feet, where she squatted and wet on his shoe.

Nick hooted with laughter.

"She knows her master," Mr. Howard said, gazing at the spreading puddle.

"I'll clean it up! I'll take care of her. I'll pay for her toys and her collar, everything! If I can keep her, I'll do everything!" Gus promised.

His dad said, "Who will do it when you're at school? You know your mother's looking for a job. She's been a full-time mom long enough."

Mrs. Howard nodded. "It's true, Gus. If I get that graphic arts job I want, I'll work from nine till four."

Gus looked pleadingly at Marty. He reached into the drawer for a towel to clean up after the puppy, but his eyes never left Marty's face.

Marty shoved his glasses into place and rubbed his forehead, a sure sign he was thinking. Gus swabbed up the puddle and prayed in silence.

"Well," Marty began thoughtfully, "a lot of people who work have puppies. If they can do it, I guess we can."

Nick was now holding the puppy. "She's sure furry," he said. "Look, Mom, we'll help. We haven't had a dog in a long time. She could stay in the laundry room when we're gone . . . with papers on the floor."

"And as soon as I get home I'll clean up and put out papers in the kitchen," added Gus. "She can stay in the kitchen till she's trained. It'll work, I just know it!"

"If the roast is thoroughly dead, could we eat now?" Mr. Howard asked. "All I had was soup for lunch."

"Then I can keep her?" Gus cried.

"I guess so," his mother said. "But she's going to be the size of a moose. Look at those paws." She shook her head, resigned. "I'm putting dinner on now. Shut the doors to the kitchen to keep her in here."

"Put some papers by the door," Marty suggested. "We want her to get the idea of going to the bathroom as close to outside as we can. If I can borrow the car, I'll go to the store and get puppy food after supper."

During supper the puppy chewed everyone's shoelaces and the rag rug in front of the sink. She gnawed on Marty's and Nick's notebooks stacked by the back door. She munched the buttons on Mr. Howard's overcoat until he snatched it away and hung it up.

"Chewie will be a good name for her," Mrs. Howard said.

"How about Fuzzy?" Gus suggested.

Nick grinned. "What about Freebie? Nobody in his right mind would pay for her."

Mr. Howard spoke over the laughter. "*I'm* naming this pet. And I'm calling her Figment. I'm going to pretend she doesn't exist."

"Good lu-uck," warbled Mrs. Howard with a shake of her head. "How about some Sweet Dreams for dessert?" She set a plate of candies on the table.

"Yay!" Gus cheered, reaching for the candy. What a day. First the puppy, and now his favorite dessert.

Mrs. Thomas, the Howards' neighbor, made the Sweet Dreams in her kitchen. Her candy

making had started as gifts for friends and exploded into a business. Now there was a sign
next to her front door that said:

Rhonda Thomas, HOME-MADE CANDIES
Daily Hours: 10–4
Phone In Special Orders

Gus held the chocolate Sweet Dream on his
tongue and let its elegant flavor melt slowly.
Sweet Dreams were creamy, like fudge, but they
lasted longer. Next, he would have a Mint
Dream, then maybe a Maple. . . .

"Meow, mee-owwww," sounded from the
hallway. Paws scratched at the door into the
kitchen.

"This'll be interesting," Nick said, leaping
up from the table. "Eleanor and Fishhead and
Licky will be just crazy about our new pet."

The three cats minced into the kitchen.

"Yowp!" The puppy gallumphed across the
floor to greet them.

"SSSSS!" Three cats arched their backs, their
tails rigidly erect. "Fffft," added Eleanor, who
was the mother of Fishhead and Licky. She

lowered herself into a crouch and glared venom-
ously at the puppy.

"Take Figment for a walk," Mrs. Howard
told Gus. "Pierpont's old leash is in the laundry
room cabinet. Tie it around her neck and get
her out of here while Marty feeds the cats. They
can get to know each other later."

Gus spent that evening in the kitchen with
Figment. They had played outside in the dark-
ened backyard after supper. Then, for a time,
she had slept on his lap, her nose tucked under
his arm. He called her Figgy or Figment every
time he talked to her, wanting her to learn the
name fast. He was sure she was very smart.

After school tomorrow he would buy her a
new red collar and a matching leash. His dad
had told him to buy several chewing toys, also.

"Everything we own will be mangled before
this puppy's grown. She's the dangdest chewer
I've ever seen," Mr. Howard said. He jerked
his slippered foot out of Figment's mouth and
left the kitchen.

Gus tied knots in an old T-shirt so they could

play tug-of-war. "Figgy," Gus said, "I don't have much money. I'll bet a collar and a leash and chewy toys cost tons of money."

"Hrrr, hrrr," Figment growled joyously, her jaws clamped on the knotted shirt.

Gus watched her with love. He was going to draw her this way, her black-and-white ears flopping up and down, her fat puppy rear in the air, bushy tail waving as she gripped the shirt. Then, when she grew up, she could see how she looked as a puppy. Everyone liked to see how he looked as a baby, Gus thought. Why not dogs?

"We need money," Gus told her. "I've got to get a great idea, quick."

For a second, Figment relaxed her hold and Gus yanked the shirt out of her mouth. He threw it to the far corner of the kitchen. While she bounded to retrieve it, he checked the dessert plate and popped the last candy in his mouth.

He slid down and leaned against the cabinet to savor the Mint Dream. It was the best candy in the world.

"That's it!" he shouted.

"Yarp," the puppy whimpered, backing into the corner. She looked at Gus fearfully, her black eyes wide.

Gus rushed to comfort her. He cuddled her in his arms and whispered his great idea into one fuzzy ear.

4

Sweet Dreams

Early next morning, Gus took Figment outdoors. "You'll have a new leash and collar by this afternoon," he promised. When he talked to her, she cocked her black-and-white head to one side as if she were listening. What a perfect dog she was. Gus sat on the porch steps and congratulated himself. Figment chewed on his shoelaces.

Gus wolfed breakfast and hurried through his backyard to Mrs. Thomas's house. He pounded up her back porch steps and peered in through the kitchen window. Wahoo! She was reading the paper, her coffee cup at hand. He rapped on the window and gave her his biggest smile.

With a matching smile Mrs. Thomas opened her back door. "How's my lamb this morning?" she asked, reaching over to stroke his brown hair. She had cared for Gus for many weeks years ago, when he was two and his mother was sick. She treated him as one of her own.

"I'm super, thanks," Gus said. She was pretty good about calling him her "lamb" only when they were alone, not in front of his friends. She was just like a third grandma.

"You need something, don't you," Mrs. Thomas observed.

Gus nodded. "I got a dog! Did you see her in our yard just now? Her name's Figment. Isn't she great?"

"I thought that was a new animal at your place."

"Right," Gus said, racing on, "and she needs chewy bones and a collar and leash and I want to pay for them so can I buy some Sweet Dreams?"

"Just slow down a bit. And yes, you can have some Sweet Dreams."

While Mrs. Thomas boxed four dozen Sweet Dreams, Gus explained. He wanted to buy four dozen every day, in assorted flavors. He would put two each in separate little bags himself, and charge forty cents a bag.

Mrs. Thomas stopped boxing candies. "You mean you're going to charge *more* for them at school?"

"Sure! I'll be the only one who's got any! That makes them cost more, see? It's my commission. The people who sell my dad's computers get a commission. It's only fair!"

"But these are my special candies, Gus. Everyone knows what they cost—a dollar twenty-five a dozen. I don't like to overcharge, dear."

Gus tried to be patient. His mom always said you had to be patient with older people. "I know, but I'm bagging them and taking them to school. That's worth extra!"

She nodded—reluctantly, he thought. "Well, we'll see how it goes. Now Gus, are you allowed to do this? Sell food on the school grounds?"

"Sure. Why not?" Gus tucked the box of candy into his backpack next to the bags he had brought from home. He got out the birthday five-dollar bill he'd been saving for months. He admired its crisp newness for the last time as it disappeared into Mrs. Thomas's bathrobe pocket. This idea better work, he thought.

At school, Gus had only ten minutes before the bell. He hustled into the boys' bathroom and locked himself in the large, enclosed stall in the corner. He put twenty-four bags in a pile, putting two candies into each bag. It took forever to wrap all the twist-ties, but at last he had all twenty-four bags ready to go, inside a paper bag.

Gus slid into his seat just as the bell rang. Hah! he thought. I'm in business. If I sell all the bags at forty cents a bag . . . His forehead wrinkled as he worked the arithmetic in his head.

"Nine dollars and sixty cents!" he said, seeing a profit of four dollars and sixty cents.

Pepper turned around to ask, "What's nine

dollars and sixty cents? Where were you this morning?"

"No talking, guys," Mr. Keene said. "Everybody get out your papers on Africa. First we're going to make our sentences into good sentences, okay? Then we'll copy them over so I can put them up on our bulletin board."

Gus tried to concentrate on good sentences, and then on reading, until time for recess. What if only a few kids had money? Of course, those who lived nearby and went home for lunch could bring money for the afternoon. What if the candies were being squashed in his backpack?

When the recess bell rang, Gus pulled the paper bag out of his backpack, put on his parka, and got ready to open his candy store.

"Sweet Dreams? No joke?" Pep exulted when they got outdoors. "I'll take three bags."

"They're forty cents a bag," Gus told him.

"Whoa! Hey, that's too much!"

Gus shrugged. "Can't help it."

Pep frowned and counted his change.

"What's in the bag?" Buzzer asked.

Gus sold two bags to Pep and one to Buzzer. "Best candy in the world," Buzzer said.

Word spread. Gus had a crowd in no time. He thought he had sold about eighteen bags when the playground teacher started moving toward them.

He remembered Mrs. Thomas's question. Maybe—he didn't know why—but maybe the school wouldn't like his selling candy on the playground.

"Take off," Gus told the knot of kids around him. "Here comes Old Bush-Face. See me after lunch, okay?"

Old Bush-Face was an older woman teacher—older than Mr. Rawson—older than the school maybe. Above her upper lip was a dark line of hair, rather like a man's mustache. Gus's oldest brother Jut had told him, "She's a good teacher, but strict. Nobody gets away with anything around her."

The kids scattered as Old Bush-Face, really Mrs. Evanston, strode over to Gus. "What's so exciting over here?" she demanded.

Gus shrugged. "I just shared some candy.

41

Probably ruined everybody's lunch, hunh?"

Mrs. Evanston narrowed her eyes. "Probably. Well, run along and play now. That's why we're all out here."

Gus smiled innocently, clutched his candy sack to his chest, and took off for distant parts. He was afraid that Old Bush-Face hadn't believed him. Sure hope I don't get her for sixth grade, he thought.

Buzzer bought a very small lunch to save money. After lunch, he paid Gus another forty cents for one more bag of Sweet Dreams.

"Wouldn't you like to share with an old, old friend?" Pep suggested.

"Nope." Buzzer popped a Maple Dream into his mouth.

Gus was pocketing the last forty cents for the last bag when he heard footsteps—big, adult footsteps—marching down the corridor.

"Get out of here," he whispered to his customer, a sixth-grader named Jerry Somers. Without even turning around he knew it was Mrs. Evanston.

"Stop right there," she told Jerry.

Jerry panicked. He stuck the bag of candy under one arm and clamped that arm to his side.

"I saw that," Mrs. Evanston said. "Show me what you hid under your arm, please. Right now."

Jerry sent a despairing look Gus's way and said, "Yes, Mrs. Evanston." He held out the bag.

She looked at the candies, then at Gus. "Why is this a secret? Did you just give these candies to Jerry?"

Gus thought of the nine dollars and sixty cents in his jeans pocket. He wished he had had the brains to open his candy shop in the boys' john. Why had he let kids buy candy in the hall outside the lunchroom? Dumb! he thought.

"I'm waiting, Gus," Mrs. Evanston said.

"He's been sharing it with kids all day," Jerry volunteered, looking at the floor, not at Mrs. Evanston.

"Is that true?" she asked Gus.

He sagged under her gaze. "Well, sort of," he began. "I was starting a business, see, because I've got a dog now. She needs a collar and a leash and some chewy bones—all kinds of stuff that costs tons of money."

"Then you sold these bags of candy?"

"I thought it was a good idea," Gus said weakly.

"Who is your teacher?" asked Mrs. Evanston.

In an instant, or so it seemed to Gus, he was standing in front of Mr. Keene's desk. Mrs. Evanston explained why.

"I expect you will handle this," she told Mr. Keene as she left the room.

When Mrs. Evanston had gone, Mr. Keene allowed himself a smile. Then he looked at Gus. "Big boo-boo," he said. "You can't sell food on school grounds. Didn't you know that?"

Gus shook his head.

"Okay, then. But no more. I don't want you to land in the principal's office again." He pulled out one of the papers on his desk. "This is your paper on Africa, and it's terrific. Now I can't have one of my best students in trouble all the time, can I? It makes me look terrible. I'm new to fourth grade, too, you know."

Gus relaxed. "Okay. I just thought it was a good way to earn money and make everybody happy."

"Are you saying you sold the candy at a discount?"

"Well, no," he admitted.

"I guessed as much. Anyway, Mr. Salesman, that phase of your life is over." He paused, pulling at one earlobe, studying Gus. "I hope you're planning to spend time with your puppy—training her and grooming her. It'll keep you busy, know what I mean?"

Gus grinned. He knew what his teacher was politely not saying. But life goes better when I keep thinking of interesting things to do, Gus decided. Lately I haven't been bored for a minute.

5

Fooling Miss Pooley

Right after school Gus bought a red leash and matching collar and two rawhide chewy bones. He and Pep planned to take Figgy for her first real walk. Buzzer, grumbling constantly, was headed for a dentist appointment.

"Only fifteen cents left," Gus said as they headed for home. Of course, Figment deserved the best. Now he could draw her wearing her new collar, maybe bouncing along at the end of the red leash.

" 'Bye," Buzzer said gloomily at his corner.

"Once," Gus told him, "Dr. Purdy had an emergency, so I didn't have my appointment. Maybe you'll get lucky."

"I'm never lucky," Buzzer said.

At home, Gus found his mother in the backyard. "Good dog, Figgy!" she was saying.

"What's going on?"

"That." His mother pointed. "You get to clean it up. But she came outside to do it, so we should be grateful."

"Thanks, but you didn't have to take her out, remember?"

Mrs. Howard pulled off her scarf and started for the house. "I know, but I can't relax till an animal's trained."

Gus cleaned up after Figment and put on her red collar. She sat down and pawed at it unhappily.

Pep biked into the Howards' driveway minutes later and the boys snapped on Figment's new leash. The puppy turned to chew on it. She wouldn't go anywhere.

Gus removed the leash from her mouth and dragged her toward the sidewalk.

"We're supposed to go *fast*," Pep said. "So I can run."

"Come on, Figgy," Gus urged. "Quit sitting down all the time." He turned to Pep. "Did you hear we're starting cooking tomorrow? I hope it's better than sewing was."

"That whole idea is dumb," Pep said, jogging away.

"My mom thinks it's terrific. She says when she's working she won't have time to sew on everybody's buttons or make all the snacks we want."

Gus soon tired of dragging Figment and yelling ahead to Pep, who was getting farther and farther away. "This is enough!" he hollered. "Let's go play Monopoly."

The next afternoon, part two of Program Independence began in Gus's class. Part one had been the sewing that he and Pep disliked. Nonetheless, the Hampshire Middle School was determined to teach the basics of sewing and cooking. For one ninety-minute period a week, every class practiced its domestic skills.

"You all behave," Mr. Keene warned as he left the room. "Miss Pooley's a professional dietician and she's doing the school a favor. I expect you to listen politely."

Miss Pooley was a thin, jumpy lady who wrung her hands as she looked at the class. "We'll be cooking next week, but first I want to discuss the different food groups." Her voice quivered and she kept twisting her hands together.

Gus whispered, "Do her hands itch or what?"

"You've got me," Pep mumbled back over his shoulder. "This's gonna be worse than sewing."

Nanny Vincent's hand flapped in the air. "Miss Pooley, I can't hear. Those boys are talking." She made a face at Gus and Pep.

Gus pulled down one corner of his mouth and let his tongue loll out while he screwed up his eyes and squinted at Nanny. "Aaaah," he groaned. Just like the Creature from the Black Lagoon.

"Children, children!" begged Miss Pooley. The kids giggled loudly.

The door burst open and Mr. Keene sprang into the room. "That will be enough of that!" he roared.

Mr. Keene never roared. Each student sat up straight.

"I ordered you to behave yourselves and I meant it," he went on grimly. "I will be watching, understand? Anyone causing trouble will stay after school FOR A WEEK."

Twenty-two heads nodded like puppets. Twenty-two awed voices said, "Yes, Mr. Keene."

Oh brother, Gus thought, slumping down in his seat. He heard soft sighs from around the room.

Miss Pooley began with the glories of Bread and Grains, one of the four food groups.

Gus began to draw, glancing up now and then. When he saw Mr. Keene peering in the window, Gus fixed his eyes on Miss Pooley.

Somewhere in the next food group, Dairy Products, Gus knew that his drawing stank. He wadded it into a tight little ball. That was when the idea struck.

In his mind he could hear Nick. "No lie,"

Nick was saying, laughing as he talked. "You chew till it's real soggy. Takes a couple minutes. Then wad it into a ball and heave it up there. It'll stick. It'll stick forever."

Gus looked up at the tile ceiling. Mmhmm, worth a try. He slipped the paper wad into his mouth and began chewing.

"Because your bones and teeth need calcium, you should drink milk every day," Miss Pooley lectured.

Gus chewed on in spite of the acky taste. He propped his face in his hands, hoping no one would see his jaws moving. It sure did take a long time.

Gradually, the paper began disintegrating into bitsy pieces. *Now,* he thought, gagging. While he molded the soggy wad into a loose ball, he made sure that Mr. Keene was not in sight. Miss Pooley was writing on the chalkboard. Nanny Vincent was taking notes.

Phoom! Up went the wet paper. It hit the tile ceiling . . . and stuck. Gus smiled.

He glanced around the room, just in case anyone had been watching. Buzzer was staring at him, eyes wide. He pointed up at the paper wad. "How?" he mouthed.

Gus explained how on a tiny piece of paper. He added, "I bet I can get more balls up there than you." When Miss Pooley's back was turned, he sent the note on its way.

Miss Pooley stopped writing and turned to the class. "Are there any questions on the first two food groups?"

No one had a question. Not even Nanny Vincent.

"Then we'll move on to Meat and Fish," said Miss Pooley.

Gus passed another note to Pep, straight ahead of him. Pep checked out the ceiling, grinned over his shoulder at Gus, and began crumpling a piece of paper.

Buzzer's jaws moved rhythmically up and down, up and down, although he was frowning terribly.

It really is gross, thought Gus, chewing a new wad.

Buzzer was extremely careful. He waited until Miss Pooley was again writing on the chalkboard. Then, *phoom!* It flew up . . . and stuck. He grinned across the room.

Nanny looked up from her notes and saw Buzzer's smile. Her pale eyes darted across to Gus—then back to Buzzer, who was still grinning. There was nothing to smile about in the Meat and Fish group. Nanny's eyes zeroed in on Gus again.

Uh-oh, he thought. She knows something is up. He was careful not to move his jaws. He kicked Pep's leg in warning. Pep jerked upright and froze.

"You must remember," Miss Pooley said, "to buy fresh meat and fish and to store them properly."

This is nuts, Gus thought. Kids don't buy groceries.

Even Nanny Vincent looked bored. She stopped examining Gus and Buzzer and slipped a book out of her desk.

Hah! Gus thought. Now I could tell on *her*! He tried to imagine himself saying, "Miss Pooley, Nanny's reading a book instead of paying attention."

Nah. He couldn't do it. Also, his mouth was full of gummy paper. Just then he saw Pepper's hand fly upward. Another wad stuck on the ceiling. Now they each had one.

Nanny's hand waved frantically. "Miss Pooley? Pepper's doing something. So is Gus. And Buzzer. I just know it."

Pep looked scornfully at Nanny. "I put up my hand to ask a question." He smiled at Miss Pooley. "How can we know when meat and fish are fresh? I got food poisoning once, and man, was I sick!"

Miss Pooley gave Pep her full attention. "Oh, I'm sure you were sick, you poor boy. Food poisoning is dreadful." She began explaining how fresh meat looked and smelled.

Nanny broke in, whining. "But Miss Pooley, I know—"

Mr. Keene strode into the room. "Do you have a problem, Nanny?" he growled.

Nanny withered in her seat. She put one hand over the book on her desk. "No," she said in a small voice.

"Good," he growled again. He looked up and

down the rows. "No funny business," he warned. "Miss Pooley is donating her time, as I said, and she deserves our respect."

Gus was afraid he'd have to swallow his paper, but Mr. Keene finally left. When Nanny looked down at her desk, he spat the awful wad out of his mouth.

Miss Pooley had moved to Fruits and Vegetables, the last of the food groups, before Gus got another chance. He let it fly. The paper wad sagged slightly, but it held, and he gazed at it with pride. Now he was two to Pep's and Buzzer's one apiece.

He looked down at his desk to find a note stuck under the edge of his paper pad.

"You win," it said. "Keene's twitchy today. I quit." It was signed with a P for Pepper.

Gus looked over at Buzzer, who was making "No way!" signs with his hands. Buzzer leaned back in his seat and pretended to be sleeping.

Gus began drawing Miss Pooley, the lady who was doing them such a wonderful favor. At least they'd be cooking the next time she came, not hearing a long lecture.

Cooking, Gus mused as her reedy voice droned on. There ought to be some way to make cooking more interesting.

That afternoon Gus tried again to take his dog for a walk. And again she sat down . . . or chewed the leash . . . or chewed his shoelaces. She ran circles around him, wrapping the leash about his ankles. They didn't even get as far as the corner of their block. "I give up," Gus said.

Inside the backyard, Figment took off, a blur of black and white. Gus sat on the top porch step with his pad of paper. He wanted to draw her this way—free and full of joy. The picture should show her puppy heart.

He ruined four pieces of paper before he had a drawing he could accept. By then his hands were blue with cold. He held the drawing out and examined it critically. Not Michelangelo, that's for sure. But drawing dogs was probably harder than painting ceilings.

The door creaked and his mother stuck her head out. "Come inside, okay? I have something exciting to tell you."

As he stepped indoors, she said, "I got the job! They just called and I start on Monday. Can you believe it? I'm going to phone Dad and tell him to buy steaks. Do you remember when Nick and Marty are getting home? This calls for champagne, don't you think?" She paused, breathless.

"Chill out, Mom. You'll pop before Monday gets here."

"Oh, Gus, don't be a wet blanket. Please!"

"Pep says moms shouldn't work. His mom doesn't."

Mrs. Howard made a face. "Look, Gus, I've been at home for twenty years. I can bake brownies blindfolded. I'm bored to tears. You, of all people, should understand when somebody's bored!"

You got me there, he thought, unzipping his parka. More than anything I hate being bored. "Sorry. What is your job, anyway?"

"Now that's more like it! I'll be doing ads and company brochures—designing them, editing them—what I studied in college." Her brightness faded. "Except it'll be hard. I've forgotten so much, and it's all different now. I'm amazed they're giving me a chance."

"But you're great! I couldn't draw anything till you showed me." He held out the new drawing. "See? This isn't too bad, is it?"

She studied the picture. "You've always been better at animals than I am. But look . . ." She grabbed a pencil and made a few strokes on the drawing. "You have to let us feel what's under the fur—the bones and muscles we can't see. An artist has to know where they all are and what they do."

He saw the difference a few lines had made. "How'd you know to do that?"

"Art classes. I've always taken classes, you know. It's why I'm not a raving loony." She grinned.

"Were there any boys in those classes?"

"Of course. More men than women in my class in England. Now I'm going to call Dad, Gus. I can't wait one more second!"

Before dinner that night, the Howards celebrated with champagne. Gus gave his to his dad. "It's kind of soury. Can I have a Coke?"

"We can buy a cabin at the lake now, right, Mom?" Nick looked hopefully at his mother.

"First we need a car for the teenagers," said Marty.

"Yeah! And one for Jut so we don't have to pick him up when school's out," added Gus. Even though Jut was his favorite brother, and he could hardly wait for Easter when he would be home, Gus hated the long ride to Illinois, where Jut was a junior at Northwestern.

Mr. Howard began to laugh. "Even your mom can't earn money that fast." He smiled at her. "I hope you're going to get some help around here. Otherwise, you'll be working night and day. That's no fun."

"Right! A maid, a cook, and a butler. Cool idea." Nick grinned at Marty. "No more chores."

"No cook," Marty said. "Gus's learning how."

Gus frowned. "No I'm not. She just blabbed about food groups today. Buzzer said we're making scrambled eggs next. Barfo. Who cares about eggs?"

6

Gus Howard, Master Chef

In the days following his mom's big announcement, Gus concentrated on Figgy. He wanted her to walk on the leash and to use the outdoors as her bathroom. Figment wasn't sure she liked either of those ideas.

Before Gus or any of his classmates were ready, Miss Pooley returned to their school. She stood in front of them again, wringing her hands as before. She was wearing her coat and a weird purple wool hat.

"I wouldn't wear that hat if we lived at the North Pole," Gus whispered to Pep.

"Please get into your coats for our walk to the junior high," she quavered. "We have their home ec lab today so that we can learn to make omelettes."

Omelettes! thought Gus. Now that's more like it.

"Buzzer must have been wrong about scrambled eggs," Pep said as they pulled on their coats. "I love omelettes. This'll be great."

Pep set the pace and the fourth grade jogged the block to the junior high. Miss Pooley, purple hat flopping, panted at the back of the group.

In the home ec kitchen, she let the class divide itself into three groups of four and two groups of five students. Their recipe was called "Omelette Surprise."

"The surprise is what you put into your omelettes," Miss Pooley told them. "One group may select cheese, another group diced ham, another mushrooms, and so on. Here are your choices on this counter. When you're ready, one member of each group will come here to choose your filling."

Gus, Pep, and Buzzer had Brent in their group

of four. "I hate mushrooms," Brent told them.

"That cheese looks weird," said Buzzer, peering at the different fillings. "And I won't eat green peppers."

"How about ham?" Gus suggested. All four agreed on ham.

"First," said Miss Pooley, "we wash our eggs. Select four eggs and then wash them carefully in your sink. Dry them with paper towels before you break them into the bowls."

Five students, one from each group, grabbed for eggs.

"Gus is taking all the biggest ones!" cried Nanny.

"Yeah!" chimed Bethie and Tina, Nanny's friends.

"Here!" Gus said, slamming an egg into Nanny's hand.

"Oh, ick! Gross!" Nanny bleated as egg oozed out of her hand onto her shoe and the floor.

"I'll help clean it up," Miss Pooley said, hurrying over with a rag. "All the eggs are the same size. It's silly to argue over them."

"Sorry," Gus mumbled to Miss Pooley. But

at Nanny he made his Darth Vader face with its scary, breathy sound. It was one of his best faces.

Gus's group broke their eggs into a bowl and fished out the pieces of shell. They added pepper and a seasoning salt, just as the recipe said. And last, one tablespoon of cold water.

"This is a snap," Pep said, whirling the egg-beater over his head. "Ready?"

"Hit it," Gus said after checking the recipe. "Beat till it's light in color and real, real fluffy."

Pep beat the eggs until he was red in the face. Brent beat for another minute, then Buzzer, and Gus. Theirs was going to be the fluffiest omelette in the class.

"Get the ham," Gus told Buzzer.

Buzzer came back empty-handed. "Nanny beat us. She's got it. All that's left is mushrooms and I won't eat 'em."

"Me neither," echoed Brent. "I already said that."

Gus wanted to choke Nanny Vincent. He had never known anyone who made him so mad.

"Let's look around for something else," Pep suggested. He yanked open a lower cupboard door. "Eeew, yuck!" he said, backing away.

Gus, Buzzer, and Brent bent down to look.

"Roaches," whispered Gus. "Geez, they're huge." He shuddered. Roaches were the ugliest bugs he knew.

Pep wormed his way in next to Gus. "They'd sure be a *surprise*," he whispered, giggling.

Gus knew they shouldn't do it—but he was angry. "They sure would," he agreed softly. "Get a bowl, quick."

Gus whapped four roaches on their heads with a large metal spoon. He ladled them into the bowl Pep brought and hid them under a paper towel. Brent put a saucer on top of the bowl. "Just in case they try to run away," he said.

"We aren't eating this, are we?" Buzzer asked.

"You crazy?" Gus replied, dropping margarine into their skillet. "Soon as it's hot, Pep, pour in the eggs. That's what the recipe says."

In went the eggs.

"How are you boys doing?" Miss Pooley stood

right next to Gus, who held on to the skillet.

"Just great," Gus said. "Nothing to it."

Buzzer nodded nervously, his eyes straying to the bowl with its saucer on top.

"No sweat," added Pepper. "You should help kids who need you, Miss Pooley. We're doing fine."

"Remember to lift the edges gently and tilt the skillet so that the uncooked egg runs to the bottom," she said. "Yours looks wonderfully fluffy. I can't wait to taste it." She moved over to a group at another stove.

Pep snorted and covered his mouth with his hand.

"Sssh," whispered Buzzer. "She's gonna have a fit when she sees—"

"Everything else was gone," Brent said. "I put those mushrooms down the disposal."

Oh poop, Gus thought. He'd been ready to chicken out and use the dumb old mushrooms. Just throw the roaches in the garbage. But now they couldn't. Now it was roaches or nothing. Omelette Surprise.

Pep moved next to Gus. He held the bowl

of roaches in one hand. *"Now,"* he murmured. "Nobody's looking."

Buzzer and Brent huddled around the stove, making a shield. Pep carefully laid out the four enormous roaches on one half of their omelette.

Gus tried to flop the other half of the omelette on top of them. Part flopped and part didn't.

"Cover 'em up fast!" hissed Pep and Buzzer.

Brent hopped up and down with excitement.

Gus pushed more egg mixture on top of the roaches. One roach rear end still showed.

Pep reached into the skillet and pushed egg on top of it with his finger. "Ow!" he hollered, snatching his hand away.

Miss Pooley dashed over. "Do you have a problem?"

"No problem," Gus said. "Pep got a little burn, but it's nothing. We're almost done."

"My, yes," she said, looking at the skillet. "Yours is by far the fluffiest! Bring it into the next room as soon as you're finished. Everyone else is waiting."

Gus carried their omelette into the next room.

"On the table here, with the others," directed Miss Pooley. "You see, class, what I meant about fluffy? This one is a beauty!"

Brent giggled. Buzzer looked as if he might be sick.

Gus glanced at Pep and decided that even he was getting worried. The class stood around the large table to watch.

One by one, Miss Pooley cut into each omelette to expose the surprise. "Nanny, your group should have beaten yours longer, but it will be good anyway. Ham omelettes are a real favorite. Maybe you could make one now for your family?"

"Maybe," Nanny said, frowning. "You never said how long we should beat it."

Miss Pooley poised her knife and fork over the last omelette. "This one must be mushrooms," she said, slicing carefully.

Floop! went her knife and the omelette lay open. There they were—four roaches in an eggy grave.

Some kids screamed and jerked backward. Gus, Pep, Buzzer, and Brent stood frozen in place. The roaches looked dreadful in all that nice egg—in the fluffiest omelette of all.

"Surprise?" Gus said weakly.

The kids began to laugh. Some boys staggered around the room, holding their sides and howling.

"Is this a joke?" Miss Pooley asked, her voice shaky.

Gus began to admire Miss Pooley. *She* hadn't screamed or jerked backward. She wasn't bawling them out or threatening to call the principal, either.

"It . . . it was a joke, sort of," Gus began awkwardly. "See, we all hate mushrooms and that was all that was left."

"So we checked the cupboards," Pep interrupted. "We'd have been okay with some old cheese. Anything! But this is what we found."

"Maybe it isn't as funny as we thought," Gus went on. "We had a great omelette. . . ." His voice trailed off. Boy, they were in trouble now. When Mr. Rawson heard about this, they were in for it.

Miss Pooley managed a smile. "Well, everyone

said I was going to learn a lot teaching." She looked at Gus's group. "But I don't need any more surprises like this one, okay?"

Gus, Pep, Buzzer, and Brent nodded solemnly.

"Promise?" she insisted.

"Yes, Miss Pooley," they said together.

Nanny fixed Gus with a pale stare. "I'm telling," she began.

"No!" said Miss Pooley, without a quiver. "This is my class. What we do here is my business, Nanny. It was a joke and that's the end of it. Next time we're going to make pizza— *without mushrooms!*"

7

The Return of
the Salesman

Several days went by and Gus stayed out of
trouble. He kept trying to take Figment for
walks and he drew more pictures of her. Right
now, he thought, before she grows up. A kid
really ought to get a fresh puppy every year
on his birthday. He spent a long time drawing
her plush black-and-white coat. He was careful
to show her feet getting bigger. When she slept,
worn out from playing, he held her, his hands
nestled in her thick coat.

He had decided that his teacher and the principal were not going to hear about the roach om-

elette. Then, on a Friday afternoon, Mr. Keene asked him to stay after school.

As she left the classroom, Nanny Vincent made a ha-ha face at him and Gus knew. She had tattled after all.

Gus moseyed up the aisle to sit across from Mr. Keene's desk.

"So . . ." Mr. Keene began. He ran a hand through his curly hair, messing it up even more than usual.

"So," echoed Gus. He smiled.

Mr. Keene smiled back, then stood up and began pacing the front of the room. "You know, Gus, you remind me of myself when I was your age. We're a lot alike."

"We are?"

"Yes, very much. Once in junior high, when I took a semester of home economics, we had to make a cake. My group cut up several pieces of pink bubble gum and put it in our cake." He chuckled. "You should have seen the teacher's face when she cut a piece and all those gooey, pink strings hung down from her knife." He shook his head, remembering.

73

Gus nodded. "Who told you? Nanny?"

"Who else?" He sat down in the seat next to Gus. "I think I'm beginning to figure out why. She's jealous."

"Of me?" Gus's voice rose, unbelieving.

"You bet. See, you know how to have fun and I'm not sure she does. You go around looking pleasant, like somebody who'd be nice to know. It's a great habit, Gus, and I don't think she's learned it yet."

Gus didn't know what to say. He just nodded again and waited.

"She doesn't have much confidence in herself, Gus, even though she's a bright student. You've gotten the best of her at times this year—with grades, and with a few pranks. She probably doesn't like that much."

"Geez! I can't help the grades!"

"Of course not. But it makes her angry and so she waits for a chance to get back at you."

"She sure does! Miss Pooley told her not to tell, too. Miss Pooley wouldn't nark on somebody."

"Right. She said your group made a very

nice pizza, by the way. She said you guys tended to business this time and had the best crust in the class. I need that recipe, okay? My pizza crust is always soggy."

"Pep and I tossed ours around in the air a lot, like they do at real pizza places. We dropped it a couple times but nobody saw us, so it was okay."

The teacher grinned. "A hot oven kills most anything. Look, Gus, I want you to think about what I said. And before you go, would you check out our ceiling?"

Oops! Gus looked up, knowing what he would see. There they were—dried paper blobs on the white tile squares of the ceiling. He looked at Mr. Keene. "It was when Miss Pooley was going on and on about the food groups," he began.

"I thought so. How did you ever get that little trick past the eagle eye of you-know-who?"

"It wasn't easy. She knew we were doing something, only she couldn't figure out what. She was getting close, though, so we quit."

"Smart move. Well, *no more*, hear? Now hop

up on my shoulders and reach up there and get that junk off my ceiling. Then you can go home."

Buzzer and Pep had gone ahead, so Gus walked home alone. That was okay. He was working on a new idea—how to buy more chewy bones for Figment. And another leash. She had nearly chewed through her brand-new red one.

He walked slowly. Money. He needed money again. Maybe he could borrow from Nick or Marty? Nah. Bad idea. Nick and Marty bugged him every minute when he owed them money. Anyway, Figment was his dog. He should figure out how to pay for her stuff.

He could do extra jobs around the house— especially now that his mom was working and needed help. Barfo and more barfo. He did enough at home already. Besides, his mom was getting a lady to help as his dad had suggested.

Gus cleaned up after Figment and ran around the yard with her awhile. He rode his bike over to Pep's house, and then to Buzzer's. They all biked out to the park, even though it was winter.

"Still no ice," Buzzer said, gazing at the lake. "If it'd just get colder, we could ice skate."

"It's February already. Pretty soon we can forget it," said Pep. "Come on, let's race to my house."

Part of Gus rode his bike and part of him didn't. His mind was off somewhere working on an idea to earn money.

"How can I earn some money?" Gus asked Marty that night after dinner.

Marty shrugged. "You've got me. Just don't ask for a loan because I'm short, too."

"Can't you see I'm busy?" Nick said when Gus wandered into his room. "I'm leaving in the morning for the weekend and I've got to finish my homework or I can't go."

Nick bent over his math book and mumbled to himself as he worked an algebra problem.

Gus was about to stomp out of the room when he saw the pencil in Nick's hand. It was shaped to fit the hand, not straight. "Where'd you get that pencil?"

Nick held it up. "Cool, huh? This kind bends. All the kids in the high school have them. Want me to get you one?"

A great idea began to rumble in Gus's brain. *All the kids in the high school have them,* he thought. Then all the kids in his school would want them, too. And if he could sell them . . .

Gus tried to stay calm. "Thanks, but maybe I'll buy one sometime. Where'd you get it?"

"Markham's Office Furniture and Supply, downtown. It's the only place that sells them. Look, Gus, I have to—"

"I'm going, I'm going!"

And on Saturday he went—to Markham's with his week's allowance plus all of next week's.

"Pencils are twenty cents each," the clerk said. "Or two dollars for a box of twelve. That saves you forty cents."

Gus said, "You're sure this's the kind that bends?"

The clerk smiled. "That's what I've heard. We can check, just to be sure." She pressed on one wooden pencil in a few places, then held it up. "Silly thing looks like an S-curve. Is that what you want?"

"Yes, please. I'll take three boxes." He paid the clerk six dollars plus tax.

When Gus got home he tucked the pencil boxes into his backpack, ready for Monday morning. He would sell them for thirty cents each and his six dollars would become ten dollars and eighty cents. Magic!

He did some more arithmetic. If I do this *again*, he thought, I'll have twenty-one dollars and sixty cents. Oh yeah. I have to subtract what I pay for the pencils. He subtracted twelve dollars plus tax from twenty-one dollars and sixty cents. Okay. About nine dollars. More than enough to buy chewy bones and a new leash.

The school won't care, Gus told himself. Pencils aren't like candy. Pencils are for schoolwork.

Monday morning, Gus sold four pencils on the way to school—two to Buzzer and two to Pep. Both boys still had most of their allowance, which they'd gotten on the weekend.

I better sell them today, Gus thought, knowing how fast an allowance could disappear.

"You worried about something? You don't look right," Pep said as they jumped up the school steps.

"These pencils are a secret, okay?" Gus said. "It's not the same as candy, but teachers might not like it anyway. Tell the guys I'm selling them in the boys' john."

Pep grinned. "Old Bush-Face can't come in there."

"You got it," said Gus.

"All this for a dog," Buzzer said.

Recess time came and Gus opened his pencil store in the boys' bathroom. He sold two dozen pencils in ten minutes and still had a few minutes of recess.

At lunchtime, the boys in Gus's class showed other kids their bendy pencils. "See?" Brent told a fifth grader. "I made it fit my hand. Fits perfect. I'm gonna buy some more tomorrow. Mom always gives me money for school supplies."

By the end of morning recess on Tuesday, Gus was sold out. In place of three dozen pencils he had ten dollars and eighty cents in his pocket.

Mr. Keene noticed the pencils that afternoon. "Isn't that a new kind of pencil?" he asked, leaning over Tommy's desk.

Gus held his breath. Tommy was a talker. Would be just like him to say something dumb. And I warned him, Gus thought.

Tommy smiled. "Yeah, they're bendy pencils. All the high school kids have 'em."

Later Mr. Keene said, "Brent, quit fiddling with your pencil. You can bend it later when you're not taking a spelling test."

Nanny leaned across the aisle to peer at Brent's bendy pencil. Her eyes moved up the row to Stephen, who was molding a pencil to fit his hand. She poked her friend Bethie and pointed at Stephen's pencil.

"*Neither*," Mr. Keene said loudly, to get everyone's attention. "Spell *neither*."

Gus sighed as he carefully wrote *neither*. If Nanny was interested, there was bound to be trouble.

So. What could Nanny prove? Gus asked himself that afternoon as he headed home. Nothing. She hadn't seen a thing. Nobody had talked, as far as he knew.

"I'll be at your place later," he told Pep. "I'm going to buy more pencils before I go home."

"Nanny wants one," Buzzer said.

"How do you know?" Gus frowned.

"She was asking the guys at the bookstore after school," Buzzer replied. "I heard her."

"Aah, so what?" said Pep. "She's a total bowser. The boys won't tell her a thing." He pumped his legs up and down, running in place.

Gus smiled. "Good. I hope she gets real honked off, too. She told Mr. Keene about the roach omelette, you know."

Buzzer and Pep nodded glumly. "Like I said, a real bowser," Pep repeated. He began jogging. Buzzer hurried after him and Gus turned left onto Center Street to Markham's Office Supply.

Gus took three new boxes of pencils to school with him Wednesday morning. By now, all the boys in school would have heard about them. Bendy pencils were a lot more fun than regular pencils. He wanted to sell this batch quickly, before any older kids blabbed about where to buy them.

First thing, a sixth grader came over to Gus's locker. "Got any more of those pencils?" he asked.

"Ssh," Gus whispered.

"What's the secret?" the sixth grader said.

Nanny, Bethie, and Tina strolled by, eyeing the sixth-grade boy. Sixth graders were usually on the second floor.

"Meet me in the john at recess," Gus muttered. "Don't tell any girls, okay?"

"Okay, we won't tell any girls. See you later," the older boy answered cheerfully.

"Won't tell the girls what?" Tina asked.

Gus said, "I can't tell you. You're a girl."

After School

A knot of boys formed around Gus's desk before class started.

"I need some of those pencils," Carl said.

"Me, too. Mom gave me money for school supplies," said Scooter.

"Sssh," warned Gus. Through a gap in the crowd he saw Nanny eyeing them suspiciously. Boy, she was a royal pain.

"In the john," he whispered. "At recess. And don't tell any of the girls, especially Nanny."

"Sit down, everybody!" called Mr. Keene. "Right now!"

Through spelling and reading Gus wondered if he were making a big mistake. Nanny knew something was up. She didn't know what, but she would keep on until she did. That's the way she was.

I only need one more recess, he thought. Just twenty lousy minutes. So many kids want pencils I'll be sold out right away. And then I won't do it again.

As soon as the recess bell rang, Gus bolted out of his seat. He snatched his backpack out of his locker and was in the boys' bathroom like a shot.

At least fifteen boys followed him. Gus sold pencils as fast as he could make change.

"Save some for me!" Carl yelled over several heads.

"Get out of my way, kid," snarled a sixth grader. "I was in line first!"

"Shut up!" Gus hollered. "Somebody'll come in here!"

Somebody did.

"What's going on?" Mr. Keene's voice echoed off the tile walls and floor.

The crowd shrank away, edging toward the walls and the door. One boy ducked into the enclosed stall. Carl oozed behind Mr. Keene and tried to slither out the door.

"Stop right there," the teacher said, his hand gripping Carl's sleeve. "Now what the devil's going on in here?"

Gus stood alone, gripping the last box of pencils.

Mr. Keene looked at Gus, then down at the pencil box. "Don't tell me. You were selling something again, right?"

"Just pencils," Gus croaked. "Not candy. I told you I wouldn't sell candy, remember?"

"I said you weren't to sell anything. I said, 'No more, Mr. Salesman.'"

Gus felt his face heating up. "No, Mr. Keene, you didn't. You said I can't sell *food* at school. That's all. I thought, since they were pencils . . ."

"Okay. The rest of you leave now. And don't buy anything else on school property unless it's sold at the bookstore or in the lunchroom. Go on, scoot!"

The boys disappeared. The kid in the stall peered out, slid awkwardly past Mr. Keene, and escaped into the hall.

"Back to my room," Mr. Keene ordered.

Gus carried his backpack and his pencils and his anger at himself across the hall to the classroom. I'll bet Nanny told him, he thought. She probably stood in the hall and watched all those guys go into the john. I don't care if I did promise Mom, Nanny's going to be sorry.

Again, Gus sat in the seat across from Mr. Keene's desk.

"Gus, I want to make myself perfectly clear this time. You may not sell *anything* at school. Not *anything*."

"Yes, sir. I won't sell anything anymore."

"I think you knew it was wrong to sell those pencils or you'd have done it somewhere else, such as the playground. That makes me angry. So you are going to stay after school the rest of this week. And if you're not here until five o'clock every day, I will turn this over to Mr. Rawson."

Gus let out the breath he'd been holding.

"Thanks. If my folks hear from him again, I've had it."

"Mmhmm. Now tell me why you did it. Do you need money? Or was it a challenge—to see if you could get away with it?"

Gus explained about Figment. "I didn't know a dog was going to cost so much! She chewed right through the leash I bought her. And it cost a ton of money!"

"I see. Well, take the money you made from these danged pencils and buy her a lightweight chain. She can't chew through that and it's probably cheaper than a leather leash." He ran one hand distractedly through his hair. "Now run up and down this room fifteen times so you can sit through the rest of the morning."

At lunch, Pep and Buzzer tried to comfort him. "Betcha Nanny blabbed," Pep said through his sandwich. "She's a real bowser. It'd be just like her."

"What is a bowser anyhow?" Buzzer asked.

"A *dog*," Gus said, sighing. It was a dog that got him into this. Poor Figment. Every afternoon she waited for him to let her out of the laundry room. Those hours in the yard were the best part of her day. And now he'd be at school until almost dark.

"She's getting punished more than me," Gus said.

"Nanny?" Pep squeaked. "Hunh! *She* won't get punished. She never does!"

"I mean Figment. She'll think I've died or something," Gus said. "She waits all day for me to come home." She really is my very own dog, he thought. Nick and Marty don't help much. He hadn't minded until now, when he needed help.

Buzzer looked at Pep. "*We* can walk her, or let her play in your yard. If your mom says it's okay."

"Sure," Pep agreed quickly. "Figment likes us. I can run races with her. It'll be good training. I haven't been doing enough lately."

"Hey, great! How'd you guys like the rest of my pencils? I must have six or seven left anyway."

That Wednesday he stayed in his seat when

everyone else went home. He folded his hands on his desk. As long as Figment had Pep and Buzzer for company, it was okay.

Mr. Keene disappeared into the hall and came back with cleaning supplies. "You can give the janitor a break, Gus. I'll tell you what needs doing as you go along. When you finish, you can do your homework. That's what I'll be doing." He sat down with a stack of papers.

Gus was carefully brooming the window side of the room when he saw Nanny. She was under the big maple tree with Bethie and Tina. When she spied him in the window, she smiled and waved.

"Hi, Gus," she mouthed. Then she laughed. She poked Bethie and Tina and the three of them giggled and pointed at Gus, who held the broom.

Gus whirled away from the window, his face on fire. "Did Nanny tell on me?" he shouted. "Did she?"

Mr. Keene raised his head. "No. I saw all those boys charging into the bathroom and decided to see for myself. There was a lot of noise, too."

The fire in Gus's face cooled slightly. He looked at the floor, then out the window again.

Nanny waved again, happier than he'd ever seen her.

"Is she out there?" the teacher asked.

"Yup. I made her day. Her whole week, maybe."

Mr. Keene jumped to his feet. "Maybe not. My kids aren't going to gloat over others' bad luck if I can help it. You keep on cleaning. I'll be right back. Just stay out of the window for a while. That's an *order*."

Gus took his broom to the far corner of the room. Then he emptied the wastebasket into the trashcan in the hall.

He was washing the chalkboard when Mr. Keene came back. "I called your mom while I was gone," he told Gus. "She's not the happiest mother in town, but I explained why you'd been selling things, so she understands."

Mr. Keene checked his wastebasket. "Great.

I didn't even have to tell you. I really appreciate people who see what needs doing and just do it. Thanks." He sat down and began grading papers.

Gus was filled with questions. He glanced briefly out the window. No one stood under the big maple. Nanny and her friends had gone then. He studied Mr. Keene's face and decided not to ask his questions. Instead he grabbed a rag and dusted the bookshelves. He loathed dusting. But today it seemed like a good idea.

Gus hurried home in the damp, chill twilight of February. Maybe there was time to try walking Figment again. He had bought chewy bones and a chain leash at the pet store as he went through the center of town. He didn't like the chain, but it had cost less than the red leash.

Figment and Mrs. Howard were in the kitchen when he got home. His mother pointed to a chair and said, "Sit."

Gus sat. Figment began gnawing on his shoe with her pointy puppy teeth.

His mom sat down, too. "Okay. Here we

go again. Now I understand why you were selling things at school. But if you need to earn more money, I insist that you do extra jobs at home. I can use the help, and you don't want a reputation as a troublemaker at school."

"Yes, Mom. See what I got?" He held up the chain. "She can't chew this kind. It was Mr. Keene's idea."

His mother frowned. "Pencil profits?" she asked. "And that's another thing. This *family* adopted Figment and we'll pay her expenses. I see that you want to, but you don't have to. What you have to do is *stay out of trouble*."

"I promise."

She leaned forward and took Gus's hands in her own. "Gus, I really need your help now. I have to work—for me—to be happy. And I can't feel guilty about being gone from home. It will wreck everything."

"Why do you feel guilty? You didn't do anything wrong."

"When my kids act up, I feel guilty—as if it's my fault somehow. All parents are like that. We can't help it. If you keep getting in trouble, everyone will say, 'No wonder. His mother works, you know. She's never around to supervise her children.'"

"That's dumb!" Gus cried. "You get home right after I do. And you're here in the morning."

"I know, but that's what people will say anyway. And in the summer, you'll have to behave for Nick and Marty. They'll be in charge until four thirty every day."

"I'll be an angel." He held up his hand the way people did on TV in a court of law. "Hope to die."

His mom squeezed the one hand still in hers. "I'm not asking for a miracle, Gus. Just be normal, okay?"

"It's a deal. Now can I walk Figment?"

"Yes. You're going to have to be firm with her. I'll check into dog obedience classes. They're supposed to start this spring, in the evening at the high school. That'd be good for both of you."

Just then Marty exploded into the kitchen.

He was waving a piece of paper. "I got it! They accepted me! I'm in at Iowa State! Wahoo! Wahoo!"

Nick stood behind him, grinning proudly. He pounded his older brother on the back several times.

Mrs. Howard leaped up to hug him. "I didn't even check the mailbox today. Isn't it lucky you did?"

Nick snorted. "Lucky my rear! He's been living in the mailbox ever since he sent his application. Let me see the letter."

Everyone read the incredible, wonderful letter. In just a few months, Marty would begin studying to be a doctor for animals. He had never really wanted to be anything else.

Mr. Howard came in and joined the celebration.

Phew! Gus thought. Marty had saved him again. Now nobody would be mad. Well, maybe a little mad. He was used to that.

His dad came into his bedroom that night just as Gus was fading into sleep. He sat on the bed. "Mom told me about your problem at school," he said. "I had to stay after once, too. For a whole week. That was enough."

"Probably for me, too," Gus said. "I'm sorry, Dad."

"I know. Mom tells me you're starting a career as an angel. That'll be a nice change." Before he left the room, he hugged Gus hard.

9

Mister Chairman

At four thirty on Friday afternoon, Gus put the school's broom, dustrag, and sponge back in the cleaning closet. For the last time, he told himself.

Mr. Keene was admiring the classroom when Gus returned. "Our room looks terrific," he said.

"Thanks. It makes homework kind of a treat."

"Don't start yet. I want to talk to you."

"But I've been good!"

"It's not anything bad, Gus—relax. But it is important. I just heard that our school has an art show in the lunchroom every spring. Fourth-grade art is on display in early April."

"Okay." Gus waited, puzzled.

"Well, the art teacher and I agreed that you should be the show chairman for fourth grade. What do you think?"

Gus stared at him. "Mrs. Davidson said that?"

"Let's say I helped her to make up her mind."

"Oh." Gus didn't know what to think. "I—I've never seen how they do it. I was in England, remember?"

"That's okay. We decide how to do it ourselves. I'll help you and so will Mrs. Davidson."

Gus nodded slowly. "Pictures would be nice in the lunchroom. Those yellow walls are boring. But some kids can't draw *anything*."

"Right. No one is forced to enter. We'll hang only the good ones and award ribbons to the winners."

"We could have parents come for the judging," Gus suggested hesitantly. "Maybe some punch and cookies . . ."

"Terrific! You want me to play the guitar?

Sort of low, in the background? Classical stuff."
He grinned. "We'd be just like a fancy art gallery."

"Yeah! That sounds cool."

"Then you'll be our chairman?"

"Mrs. Davidson always picks girls for jobs. She likes girls."

Mr. Keene leaned forward and talked right in Gus's face. "Then it's important for us male types to show her how an art show *really* ought to be done. Right?"

Gus swallowed. "I guess so. Have you been to any art shows? I've just been to museums. They're boring."

"Gus, whatever you do will never be boring. You have wonderful ideas. That's why I wanted you to be chairman. You've already had one terrific idea—asking parents to the judging and having a reception with refreshments and music."

"Yeah. That is a good idea, isn't it?"

"You bet." Mr. Keene looked at the wall clock. "Here's another one. It's nearly five, so let's go home. Why don't we meet next Tuesday afternoon with Mrs. Davidson. Three thirty, in the art room?"

The Chairman of the Fourth Grade Art Show walked home deep in thought. How am I going to get kids to draw pictures for the show? What kind of pictures? Or posters? Kids like doing posters. Maybe we could have pictures and posters? How about clay pots? Nah. I hate little clay pots. They're baby stuff.

Gus was thinking so hard he walked smack into the kitchen door instead of opening it. When he did yank it open and walk into the kitchen, he was laughing at himself.

Mrs. Howard called out, "Hi there, whoever it is. I'm in here, collapsed on the couch."

Gus joined her in the family room. "Where's Figment?"

"She's gone for a run with Pep and Buzzer again." She yawned. "Boy, I'm beat on Fridays. Dad's bringing pizza when he comes so we don't have to cook. Did I hear you laughing when you came in?"

Gus told her why. "Our art show's going to

be great." He smiled. "Mr. Keene's just trying to keep me busy so I'll stay out of trouble."

"Clever fellow," she said lightly.

Before bed that evening, Gus counted his money. After giving the last six pencils to Buzzer and Pep and buying the chewy bones and leash, he had three dollars and ten cents. This was the week he'd get no allowance, because he had already taken it in advance. "I hate money," he said loudly.

That's a lie, he thought as he crawled under the covers. I hate trying to *earn* money when I'm just a kid. That stinks. When I'm older, I can earn as much as I want.

How? he asked as he punched his pillow into shape. Earn it how? It was the first time he had seriously asked himself what his work would be someday. It would be fun to draw all the time. Be a Michelangelo.

That made him think of the art show. Oh boy. How am I going to be a chairman? I don't even know what a chairman does. Gus pulled the sheet up over his face.

Saturday morning, as Gus poured milk on his cereal, he asked, "Nick, what does a chairman do?"

"Lots of work. Look, don't worry about that art show. The art teacher runs those things." Nick stirred his cocoa.

"But I'm the chairman! Mr. Keene said so!"

"Okay, okay! Cool your jets."

Gus gritted his teeth in frustration. "I just want to know—"

"What a chairman does," finished Nick. "All right, all right." He sipped his cocoa while he thought. "First, Gus, you make a list of the workers you need and what jobs they do. Then find people to do those jobs. All of you have lots of meetings to decide things. The chairman runs the meetings and sees that the workers do the jobs."

"What jobs?"

"I don't know! I've never run an art show!"

"It's too early to fight," Marty said as he came into the kitchen.

Nick stood up. "I'm going to watch TV.

102

Marty, tell him what chairmen do so he can run that art show."

Marty sat down at the table. "Look, Gus, you've got the best imagination in the house. Go upstairs where it's quiet and imagine the art show. See everything in place, just like you want it, okay? Then decide how it got like that. Who did the pictures? Who hung the pictures? Who got the ribbons for the winners? See what I mean?"

"That's hard."

"Yes, but you probably won't die. And your teacher will help. Now go somewhere and start imagining."

Tuesday at three thirty, Gus went to the meeting for the fourth-grade art show.

"Are you sure you want to do this?" Mrs. Davidson asked as soon as he entered her room.

She did want somebody else, Gus thought. Oddly enough, that made him more determined.

"Yes, I do," he replied. "It'll be the best fourth-grade art show we ever had."

Mr. Keene beamed at Gus.

"Well, then, let's get started," said Mrs. Davidson. "What shall we choose as our subject—our major theme?"

Gus was alarmed. He had imagined the show all weekend, and it had had many wonderful, *different* pictures and posters. "Do they all have to be about the same thing?"

"Yes. Why one particular theme?" echoed Mr. Keene.

Mrs. Davidson said firmly, "We always have a major topic or theme. It ties the show together."

Gus shifted in his chair. Art wasn't like that. Artists drew whatever they wanted. Some drew buildings. Others drew flowers. Or dogs. Something inside you told you what to draw.

"What are you thinking, Gus?" Mr. Keene asked.

"Well . . . we can't all draw about the same idea. See, I like animals and people, but my mom draws *things*. She can do animals and people better than me, but she doesn't *like* to."

"You're saying that artists are free spirits?" interpreted Mr. Keene. "That they draw best what they love, and so we shouldn't have a theme?"

Gus nodded vigorously.

"That's going to look very disorganized," Mrs. Davidson said. Her forehead was well creased.

"Maybe not," Mr. Keene said. "Our theme could be 'Free Spirit' or 'The Soul of the Artist.' Then people would understand why the pictures were all different."

"That's great," Gus said. "I like 'Free Spirit.' "

Mrs. Davidson caved in. "Well, all right, but we've always had a definite theme before."

The rest of their meeting went the same way. Gus and Mr. Keene agreed. Mrs. Davidson had other ideas. Gus won and was allowed to have posters entered in the show as a separate category. He and Mr. Keene lost when she insisted that they display all the entries, no matter how awful.

Afterward Mr. Keene walked Gus to his locker. "Well, what do you think?" he asked.

"She thinks we're crazy."

Mr. Keene smiled and shrugged his shoulders. "So?"

*　*　*　*

The end of February and all of March whisked by as Gus found out how to be a chairman.

"We need the rosettes in that window-case thing now. Right now!" he said to the Head of Awards. He had called all his workers "Head," hoping it would make them feel important. He wanted them to do their jobs.

"Why now?" complained Dana, his Awards Head. "It's just the tenth of March. The show's not till April first."

"But the window case is important! Kids need to see our winners' rosettes there so they'll want to do more pictures—or posters. Only two kids are doing posters!"

"My mom says those rosettes are gonna cost a lot more than ribbons. Who's paying for this?"

"The art department. I said that already, a long time ago. Now go get them today, okay?"

He had to convince kids to enter something in the show. "Look, Pep, you do great posters. You haven't even started yet!"

Pep shook his head. "Maybe I'll do one. But soccer's on now. That's two afternoons a week and Saturday mornings. . . ."

"His mom makes him clean his own cleats," Buzzer explained. "Every time I go over there he's messin' with his soccer shoes."

"Not all day Sunday!" Gus protested.

On the other hand, Nanny, Bethie, and Tina were drawing pictures like crazy. Nanny had already bragged about finishing three.

"I did another pastel," Tina said one March morning. "It's called *Springtime Joy*, and my mom says it's the best thing I ever did. It'll win a prize, I bet."

Gus was desperate for pictures. "That's nice," he said, even though he thought pastel chalk drawings were wimpy. He had heard that Nanny was doing a huge poster, now that she'd finished her pictures. She was extremely good at posters. As the days went by, he could tell that the class's enthusiasm was growing.

Gus saved every weekend for his own entry. He was doing a collection of drawings. They showed Figment in different poses—running, playing tug-of-war, chewing her leash, sleeping. There were seven in all, done in charcoal with red pencil for her collar.

His mother bent over the separate drawings as he shuffled them around on a large piece of paper. "A puppy collage," she murmured. "What a delightful idea. You'll redraw them then, on the big paper, when you decide how to arrange them?"

"Mmhmm, but it's harder than I thought."

"Many things are like that," she observed.

He had been right about the huge satin rosettes. The day he put them in the hall display case he drew a crowd.

"Hey, those're even better than the ones we get for band," a sixth grader said.

"Better'n winning the soccer tournament," added Pep with a frown. "Guess I better do a poster."

"Or two?" Gus suggested, closing the window to the display case. "You don't want Nanny to win for best poster, do you?"

"I heard that," Bethie piped up. "A *chairman* shouldn't say that! You're supposed to be *fair*."

"I'm not a judge!" Gus protested. "The judges pick the winners." Oops. He hadn't checked with his Head of Judges lately. How many had he found? And who were they? "Look, we need everybody to enter, okay? It'll be fair. I promise."

Gus hurried down the hall to look for Pete Johnson, the Head of Judges. Let's see, he thought. I've got to walk Figment, then call the Cookie Head. I haven't finished my own entry for the show, and next week those dog obedience classes start. Geez!

10

The Art Show

Gus examined his picture one last time. He had used his mom's words—*Puppy Collage*—as its title. He squinted his eyes and pretended he was a judge. Were the bits of red pencil for the collar in the right places? Did the puppy come alive on paper? For Gus, she did.

It's the best I can do, he thought. He covered the drawing with plastic wrap so the charcoal wouldn't smear. That morning his mom drove him to school.

"Here's my entry," he said to Mrs. Davidson

when he got to the art room. "I only had time for one."

"I'm not surprised," she said with a smile. "You've worked really hard on this show, Gus—the perfect chairman. We've never had this many pictures in a class show, nor any better ones. Just look at those entries."

"Thanks," he said, looking where she pointed. "Wooee! Tons of them!"

"Flip through them just a second before you go to class. I'm so glad the parents will be coming to see them."

That was *my* idea, Gus thought happily. Ooh, here was a zinger. It was birds in flight—sea gulls and other kinds he didn't know—with sand and windblown grasses in the background. It was called *Free Spirits*, and Amy Wright had done it. Art had always been her favorite class.

There were several wimpy pastel chalks by Tina. Many pictures of horses, all drawn by girls. Nanny's three floral arrangements—barfo. A fire truck on its way to a fire. Not bad, he thought. Bethie had done two pictures in crayon. Super barfo. But Pep's soccer poster was terrific.

And Nanny's poster about using drugs. Gus frowned at hers. It was too good. Lots of posters about bike-riding safety. And Brent's pizza poster that he'd said made him hungry all the time.

The bell rang, and Gus zipped down the hall to class. He paused at the display case to gaze at the blue first-place rosettes—one for pictures, one for posters.

By noon of the next day, April first, everything was ready. The entries in the picture contest covered two walls, with poster entries on the other two. Everyone said the lunchroom had never looked better. Later, Gus couldn't remember whether he'd eaten lunch or not.

The art show opened at four o'clock and parents began drifting in. Gus's mom and dad were there early.

"Looks terrific, Gus," Mr. Howard said. "I'm impressed. Of course, your picture's the best. We all know that." He grinned at Gus before he moved off to examine the posters.

In one corner, Mr. Keene began strumming

his guitar. Gus made sure that the lunch tables had been stacked neatly at one end, below a wall of posters. He approved the long table of refreshments—punch and cookies. His mom had made an enormous bouquet of flowers for the refreshment table, and there were napkins in the school colors, blue and white.

We did it, Gus said to himself. We really did it. "It looks good, huh?" he said to Pep.

Pep nodded. "When can we eat?"

Gus hurried over to the room mothers. Where were the judges? What were they waiting for?

As he was talking to the room mothers, Gus saw three adults enter the lunchroom with Pete, his Head of Judges. Finally, he thought, wishing he felt calmer.

Gus left the room mothers pouring punch and rushed to greet the judges.

"Let's get this straight," a white-haired judge said to Gus. "We're to give awards to the top three pictures and the top three posters?"

Gus and Pete nodded. "And two honorable mentions for pictures," Gus added. "Eight awards."

"I'm Isabella," said one of the judges, offering her hand. Gus tried not to stare. She was wearing the strangest clothes—long, balloony pants and tons of clanking jewelry. She must be the artist from Cincinnati that Pete had bragged about. "Do we announce the awards?" she asked.

Gus looked at Pete. They hadn't thought about that. "Uh . . . uh . . ." Gus began.

The third judge, a young man, spoke up. "Usually the judges make the announcement," he said. "I'm in charge of the Hampshire Museum shows, and that's how we do it."

"That's fine," Gus said quickly. They all nodded politely at one another and the judges began judging.

Gus went to stand by Mr. Keene and both watched the judges. Either they stood a long time in front of a picture or they floated by as if it didn't exist.

"They like Amy's birds," Mr. Keene said over his guitar. "Funny. Your puppy sketches show more imagination."

Gus held his breath as the judges examined his picture. Then they moved on to Tina's pastels.

"I can't stand it," Gus said. "This is awful."

Mr. Keene grinned at him. "Is this the first time you've ever entered a contest?"

"No, there's always a big parade on May Day. Kids decorate their bikes and we have bands. They give prizes, but it's different. Not like this at all."

Buzzer came over with cookies and punch. "This is for our music," he said, setting the food by Mr. Keene.

"They like Nanny's poster," Buzzer told Gus. "And she's hangin' on 'em like a leech."

Gus nodded mechanically. "How about Pep's poster? It's the only thing done in ink, and that's hard."

"I can't tell. They're just scribbling on little pieces of paper now. They figured out Nanny's listening."

Too late, Gus remembered that Buzzer had entered a picture. He hadn't wanted to. Gus had talked him into it. "Your camping picture is good, too. Those trees look real. Maybe it'll win something," he said.

Buzzer shook his head. "No way. My camp stove looks like a table and my robin looks more like a chicken. Come on, let's find Pep."

Pep was loading another plate with cookies. "Hey, this is great, isn't it?" he said. "Mom's all excited. She says we've got the best art department of any school in Ohio."

"When are the judges gonna be done?" Buzzer asked.

"Who knows?" Gus said. He felt as if he might blow apart. It was awful to care so much about winning. Now the judges were huddled over their pieces of paper.

"I'll go check," Gus said.

As he approached, the judges were nodding at one another. The white-haired man said, "We're all in agreement, how about that?"

Gus worked at sounding calm, grown up. "Should we tell everybody now?"

Isabella smiled and jangled her bracelets in the air. "I get to speak, all right, gentlemen?" She turned to Gus. "Where do you want us to stand?"

He hadn't thought of this either. "How about in front of the cookies? Then people will have to listen."

The judges followed him to the refreshment table. But now he didn't know what to do. "Just a minute," he said, leaving them to dash over to Mr. Keene. "How do I do this? It's time. They're going to tell us who won."

Mr. Keene stopped playing his guitar. "Do you want me to get everyone's attention? You look kind of strung out."

Gus nodded numbly.

Mr. Keene stood up and gave Gus's shoulder a fierce squeeze. "Yours is the best for my money, no matter what they say. And you were a terrific chairman. Come on."

Mr. Keene introduced himself to the judges. He grabbed a cup and banged it on the table while he held up one hand for attention. "It's time to announce the winners!"

When the room got quiet, Mr. Keene said, "Thank you all for coming. This is our first formal art reception—the brainchild of our chairman, Gus Howard. Let's give him a hand for doing a fine job with a difficult project."

Everyone clapped and Gus turned red. He saw his folks smiling proudly at him, his dad shaking a rah-rah fist in the air. Mrs. Davidson was smiling too and clapping hard.

"You'd probably like to thank your committee heads, Gus," Mrs. Davidson said when the clapping stopped.

Oh boy. Nobody had told him about this either. Gus pulled himself together and listed his workers, slowly, with time for clapping after each name. At the end he said, "Did I forget anybody?"

No one said anything. "That's lucky," Gus admitted, "because I didn't think about making a speech. There's a lot to being a chairman that nobody tells you."

The crowd laughed appreciatively and then Isabella took over. She said several things about how excellent the art was. At last she said, "But I'm sure you're eager to hear the winners' names." She consulted her piece of paper.

Gus stared straight ahead of him and saw nothing.

"First place for posters goes to Nanny Vincent, for *Drugs Are Demons*."

Much applause surrounded Nanny as she stepped forward, glowing, to receive her blue rosette.

"The judges especially liked this entry," Isabella went on, "because of its imaginative demons."

Dimly, Gus saw Nanny showing the big blue rosette to her mother and her friends.

"Second place for posters goes to Pepper Browning, for *Soccer Tournament*, the only work in ink, which we felt was superbly done."

Pep came forward for his red rosette. Gus leaned over to say, "Yours was the best," as Pep nodded to the crowd.

"Third place for posters goes to Brent Halliday, for *Pizza Time*, which made all of us hungry." Isabella gave the white rosette to Brent, who waved it in the air.

"And now the awards for pictures."

Gus gazed at the floor. He tried to tell himself that winning didn't matter, but he knew he was lying.

"First place goes to Amy Wright, who expressed the theme of the show with her lovely birds, *Free Spirits*."

More clapping. Amy stepped forward, her face all blotchy and funny. Gus could tell she was about to cry. He hoped he didn't.

"Thank you so much," Amy said, her voice unsteady. She clutched the blue rosette to her chest.

Gus felt Mr. Keene's hand on his shoulder.

"Second prize for pictures goes to a delightful grouping in charcoal and pencil, *Puppy Collage*, by Gus Howard. Seems to me we've heard that name before." Isabella's bracelets clinked as she held forth the rosette.

He walked around Mr. Keene to Isabella and the red rosette. It was a handsome award. He should be "thrilled to death," as his mom would put it. But he had wanted the blue one. First place. He had imagined it on his picture at home—maybe in the family room. The blue rosette, not the red one that meant second best.

"Thank you," he said to the judges. He went back to his place next to Mr. Keene.

"Next year," Mr. Keene whispered. "The blue one."

The third-place rosette went to Tina for *Springtime Joy*, her pastel chalk drawing. Dana won a green honorable mention ribbon for her drawing of kittens in a basket.

And then Nanny Vincent was coming forward again, wearing her blue first-place rosette on her blouse.

Gus jerked to attention. He watched her accept the other honorable mention ribbon for one of her pictures of flowers. She floated back into the crowd, but not before waving the ribbon in Gus's face and mouthing "Ha, ha" as she went past him.

"If it's any comfort," Mrs. Howard said on the way home, "I think yours was the best of the pictures."

"Of course it was," echoed Mr. Howard. "I said that right at the beginning."

"You're my parents," Gus said. "You're on my side."

Mrs. Howard shook her head. "But today

I was using my artist's eye. Judges differ, you know. In college shows I used to win with some judges and not even place with others. Judges have subjects they prefer. And Amy's picture was extremely good, even if it wasn't original."

Gus said, "Uh-huh."

"Her mother told me she's taken lessons for years," Mrs. Howard went on. "At the museum. Mrs. Wright thinks their teachers are excellent."

"Well, geez!"

Gus's dad chuckled. "Seems almost like cheating, doesn't it? Of course it isn't. And yours was a winner, too. The judges said so. You be sure to take Jut to see the exhibit when he's home next week for Easter, okay?"

Gus looked down at the satiny red rosette. This was his award and it was very special—just not the one he'd wanted.

Pep and Buzzer came over to Gus's house after dinner a few days later for a Friday-night sleepover.

"Mrs. Davidson put up little gold signs today

on each picture that won an award. After lunch. Did you see 'em?" asked Buzzer.

"No," Gus said. "But she told me she was going to. Nanny has two, doesn't she?"

"Yup." Buzzer took another handful of popcorn from the bowl. "She's the only one with two."

Gus chomped on a popcorn old maid and bit his cheek. "Poop!" he yelled.

"She's a poop, you bet," Pep said.

"A real bowser," added Buzzer. "And she never quits."

"We ought to be able to think of *something*. Come on, Gus. Somehow, we gotta get her," urged Pep.

Gus was dying to get her. He had known he would be sorry if he promised his mom to leave her alone. Well, now he was sorry, all right, because it was *impossible* to ignore Nanny Vincent. She made it impossible.

"She's been asking for it all year," Gus said.

"Count me in," said Buzzer.

11

WANTED: One Great Idea

A week after the art show opened, Jut came home from the university for Easter break. It was such a short holiday he had taken an airplane to save time.

Gus took him to school to see the art exhibit.

"Great stuff," Jut said as he walked from one picture to another. He stood a long time in front of *Puppy Collage.*

"Now we know who got Mom's talent," he said, smiling down at Gus. Jut was six feet tall, as tall as their dad. In junior high he'd told everyone he was going to be a shrimp. "You must have a good art teacher here."

"Yeah . . . and Mom taught me a lot, but there's *more*," Gus said slowly. "Tons I don't know." He stopped, sure that Jut would understand. He always did.

"You can learn. Mom did. But I don't suppose she's been pushing that, has she?"

Gus shook his head. "She's afraid to talk anybody into art because artists have a tough time making a living."

Jut admired Nanny's poster of the drug demons.

Gus made a face at the poster and turned away. "She's the biggest pain of any girl I ever knew," he said.

"How's come?" Jut asked.

Gus explained how. And when, and where, and why. "And I'm going to get her . . . somehow," he finished.

Jut grinned. "I see what you mean. Just remember this stuff up here above the eyes." He tapped his head.

"I know. That's what I'm using," Gus replied.

When they got home from school, Jut went on a walk with Gus and Figment. "She's pretty good for a puppy," Jut commented as Figment bounced along on her leash.

"She's better, but she won't heel," Gus said. "She's too young. We're learning 'come' at dog obedience school. She doesn't like that much either."

Figment stopped to investigate a bush and began gnawing on one of its twigs.

"She chewed my term paper," Jut told Gus. "Good thing it's a first draft." He draped one arm on Gus's shoulders. "Are you going to make biscuits again tonight? It's my last night, and you make terrific biscuits."

"Okay. You want pizza? Or an omelette or chili dogs? I can do those, too. We're learning great stuff."

Pep leaped down the front steps of his house and charged across the grass to join them. "Got any ideas yet?" he asked Gus. "I thought we could put Krazy Glue on her seat at school. How about that? She'd be stuck forever."

"Not in school. They'll kick me out," Gus said.

Jut chuckled. "You guys are serious, aren't you?"

"Dead straight," Gus replied. A guy in a movie had said that once.

"Buzzer's asking his sister for an idea," Pep said.

Hmmm, Gus thought. How about Nick? I get a lot of my best ideas from him. Maybe . . .

"Hey, Pep, can you come over tonight? And bring Buzzer. I think I'm sort of getting an idea."

Jut caught Gus's eye. He tapped his head as he had at school earlier that day. "Remember?" he said. "I don't want to visit my youngest brother in jail."

When Pep and Buzzer came over that night, Gus had already talked to Nick. "You're nuts," Nick had said. He had also said he would help.

Gus took Pep and Buzzer upstairs.

"Time for the powwow?" Nick asked as they piled into his room.

"Dead straight," Gus said, settling himself on the bed. "You had any ideas yet?"

Nick leaned back in his desk chair. "No. I don't know enough. When do you want to do this? And where?"

"Not at school," Gus answered quickly. "But soon."

"Yeah!" chorused Pep and Buzzer.

"Okay. How much trouble are you up for? Big trouble? Or just medium?"

Gus looked at Pep and Buzzer, who were seated on the floor by the bed.

"Oh boy," Buzzer said, shifting uncomfortably.

"They wouldn't kick me off the soccer team, would they?" Pep asked.

Gus remembered his promise again. One part of his mind kept reminding him. Mom just doesn't understand, he thought. Nanny never gives up. But if we really get her, maybe she will. Still, he did not want to be caught at it.

"I guess it better be medium," Gus told Nick.

"Right. Where does she go besides school? And we better not pull this at her house either."

Several light bulbs turned on in Gus's head. "The May Day Parade!" he shouted.

"Aah!" the other boys said at once.

"Brilliant!" added Nick, holding out an open palm. Gus slapped the palm and grinned.

"You're sure she'll decorate a bike for the parade?" Nick asked.

Buzzer shook his head. "The Girl Scouts are doing something special. I heard 'em talking at the art show with Tina's mom. She's the Girl Scout leader."

"Whose mom knows Tina's mom?" Nick asked.

"Mine," Pep said. "What good is that?"

Nick smiled. "Go call her. Ask her to find out what the Girl Scouts are doing so you guys can plan something better. She'll want you to be better, won't she?"

"Sure," Pep said. Gus took him to the upstairs phone.

"Mom knew about it already," Pep told everyone when they were back in Nick's room. "It's a caterpillar. And she already loaned Tina's mom *my* green turtleneck. Somebody's gonna be wearing *my shirt!*"

"Whoa. Start over," Nick said. "The whole thing."

Pep shook a lock of dark red hair out of his eyes and explained. "All six girls—and Nanny's one of 'em—will be under this tent thing that's a caterpillar, see? It's a sheet dyed green with a head out of papier-mâché. The girls are the legs of the caterpillar—and they're all wearing green turtlenecks and green tights." He snorted. "Just like kindergarten!"

Gus remembered their kindergarten centipede, long ago. "Yeah," he said, "but it could win a prize."

"The Mayor loves that stuff," agreed Nick. "So does the rest of the Council. Gus's right. Well, there's your idea."

"What idea?" croaked Gus.

"Whatever you do to the caterpillar," Nick said. "And remember—you never talked to me. We didn't meet in my room and I don't know anything about this. I don't need any trouble—

even medium size." He waved them out of his room and shut the door.

In Gus's room, they thought about the six-person, green Girl Scout caterpillar.

"Firecrackers, maybe?" Buzzer suggested.

"Everybody'd see us," Pep reminded him. "Maybe we could drive into 'em from the rear? Nah. That stinks too. Everybody'll see."

Buzzer said, "Let's take their sheet, the night before. Then they won't have a caterpillar."

Nobody could figure out how to steal the green sheet.

"If I could get my shirt back," Pep said, "I'd rub poison ivy all inside it. Mom didn't even ask if I wanted to let some girl use it!"

More lights went on in Gus's head. Poison ivy itched something awful. But how long did it take before somebody was itching and scratching?

"Hey, Pep, would that work? Poison ivy?"

"It works for my mom. She has to take pills if she gets it. Once she was in the hospital in bandages."

132

Buzzer frowned. "That's big trouble, not medium."

Gus knew he was right. If even one Girl Scout got sick and they found out how . . . No, it was too risky. "Really itchy," he said slowly. "That's a good idea. What makes people itch?"

"Mosquitoes," Buzzer offered. "Sunburn. Shrimp—they make me *real* itchy. I get bumps all over."

"No, dummy," Pep said, "something we can put inside their shirts and tights!"

"Gus *said*—" Buzzer began huffily.

"Okay, okay," Gus interrupted. "We just have to keep thinking of things till we get a great idea."

Time went by. Pep started to say, "Maybe we could . . ." and began yawning in the middle of his sentence. Gus and Buzzer didn't ask "Maybe we could what?" because Pep's yawn had made them yawn too.

"I gotta go home," Buzzer said. "If I'm late I get grounded. Come on, Pep."

* * * *

Days passed and the magic answer failed to come. One evening in dog obedience class, Gus saw dogs scratching themselves. Fleas! Catch a ton of fleas and . . . nah. Why would fleas stay inside clothes? They'd hop out and go hunt up a dog.

Figment plunked herself down on the gym floor and began crunching Gus's shoelace.

"Mr. Howard!" snapped the instructor. "Get your dog up off the floor!"

After class, Gus waited outside the high school for Marty to pick him up in the car.

"How'd it go?" Marty asked on the way home.

Gus petted Figment, who had draped herself all over his lap and the front seat. "Well," he said, "she always wants to play with the other dogs. That's because she's still a puppy. And she won't stop chewing."

Marty grinned. "She'll probably flunk and have to take it again. Is she learning to come?"

"Sort of. Hey, Marty, what makes people itch?"

"You mean the way fleas make dogs itch?"

"Mmhmm."

"Lice do. A kid had lice in my class once and he scratched his head all the time. Grossed me out."

"Anything else?" Gus asked hopefully.

"Poison ivy. And hives, when you're allergic to something. Dad says dry skin itches. And there's itching powder, of course. The guys say it really works, but I've never tried it. Why do you want to know?"

Gus gripped Figment's furry body. He could hardly believe what he was hearing. *Itching powder?* There was really something called itching powder? Wahoo!

"Gus? Hey? I said why do you want to know?"

"Uh, because. . . . I just wanted to know if humans had anything like fleas."

On the way to school the next morning, Gus told Pep and Buzzer about itching powder.

"Where can we get some?" asked Pep.

"Does it make people sick?" Buzzer asked.

Gus couldn't answer them. "We'll check at

the mall," he suggested. "There's tons of stores there. Weird ones, too. Nick heard one of them sells pot."

"That's one of the demons on Nanny's poster," Buzzer said. "It's mara-jew-wanna."

"Mara-wanna, dummy," Pep said, punching Buzzer's arm.

"Why don't they spell it that way then?" grumbled Buzzer.

The following Saturday, Gus and his friends rode out to the shopping mall with Mrs. Browning. "Meet me here at this entrance in two hours," she ordered. "Pepper, you pay attention to your watch, hear?"

On the top story of the mall, in a corner, they found a store called Baubles, Bangles, and Beads. A sign in its window said, "Always Perfect Party Needs." The young male clerks wore ponytails and leather vests with fringe. Their store reeked of incense.

Gus didn't see any kids inside, only teenagers and grown-ups draped in jewelry and fancy silver buttons above their tight jeans.

"Do you have itching powder?" he asked a clerk.

The clerk yawned and pointed. "Down that aisle."

They hurried down the aisle, checking both sides of the counter. Gus spotted a small tan envelope that read, "Itching Powder. Makes fleas look like amateurs." Silently, he showed Buzzer and Pep.

"Cool," Buzzer whispered. "Let's get outa here. This place is creepy."

"Chill out," muttered Gus. "How many should we get? They're really little and they cost a dollar ninety-nine, see?"

By pooling their money they had eight dollars and twenty cents—enough for three envelopes of powder and soft drinks later on.

"My whole allowance," Buzzer moaned, handing it over.

"Do you sell marijuana?" Pep asked the clerk.

"Go home, kid," snarled the clerk. "Can't you tell this store's for adults?"

The three boys raced down the mall walkway, down the escalator, and didn't stop till they reached McDonald's. Over Cokes Buzzer asked, "Do they really sell pot?"

"You can't," Gus assured him. "There's a law. Mr. Keene told us, remember? They're just trying to be cool."

"You mean weird," corrected Pep. "Let's see the itching powder."

Everyone examined an envelope. The itching powder was made of rosehips, the packet said.

"How're we gonna get it in their clothes?" Pep asked.

"Somehow," Gus said vaguely. "We'll think of a way."

"And nobody'll know we did it?" quizzed Buzzer.

"Nobody except Nanny," Gus replied, smiling.

12

May Day

Gus, Pep, and Buzzer crouched in the bushes across the street from Tina's house. It was the third afternoon they had spent in the bushes.

"The bugs are eatin' me up," said Buzzer.

"Didn't you put on bug stuff?" Gus asked, digging at a bug bite of his own. "We told you yesterday."

"I forgot. Gus, this isn't gonna work."

"It sure is boring," added Pep.

"They have to go out sometime," Gus said. "And when they do, we'll be ready. We only need a couple minutes."

"A neighbor'll see us go in, I bet," predicted Buzzer.

"Not in back where it's all bushes and trees," Gus said patiently. "Nobody can see anything back there."

"Are you real sure their stuff is *here?*" Buzzer asked.

Pep groaned. "I told you and told you! Tina's mom told my mom! They're coming here to get ready 'cause Tina's house is closest to where the parade starts. Everything's here!"

"Sssh!" Gus hissed. He was keeping quiet about his own worry. Almost no one in Hampshire locked up unless they were going away for a long time. But if Tina's family always locked their doors . . .

Just then he saw Tina bounce out the front door. Her mother followed and the screen banged loosely behind them. Gus nudged Pep and Buzzer. "This is it!"

Tina and her mom drove away in the car.

"Hurry," Gus said, leading the charge across the street. They tore around to the back of the house. Gus was easing open the back door when

Buzzer squeaked, "What if somebody's home? A gramma or a grampa?"

Gus paused. "Could we pretend we came to play?"

"Hide-and-seek," Pep said. "We'll tell 'em we're playing hide-and-seek. Now let's go!"

It was spooky being inside Tina's house when they weren't supposed to be. The grandfather clock bonged five o'clock and scared them silly.

They saw no costumes and no green sheet in the living room, kitchen, or hall. The dining room looked absolutely normal and dull.

Gus felt as if his heart had grown to fill his chest. It pounded away like a galloping horse. "In here," he panted, dashing into the downstairs den.

There it was. The green sheet had been sewn to wire supports to resemble the top of a caterpillar. It stretched along one wall, its head resting in the corner. Next to it was a box of green clothing.

"Be careful," Gus said. "Take two shirts and two tights and don't use up all your powder.

Make it last so we get everything. And hurry!"

"In the armpits," Pep suggested. "And around the neck."

"Feet, too," Gus said, worming his hand into a pair of tights. "That's awful. I hate it when my foot itches."

Nervous sweat dripped down his face. He had thought this part would be funny. They'd be laughing like crazy while they put itching powder in Nanny's clothes. That's what he had thought. But the reality was different.

"What's this stuff gonna *do*?" Buzzer asked. "Will they run around scratching and yelling? Is that what it does?"

"Sure," Gus answered, faking confidence he didn't feel.

The clothes were all over the floor when they finished. Gus made them fold each shirt and pair of tights carefully. "It's got to look the same as when we found it," he insisted. "Moms can always tell.

"Was it here? Right by the sewing machine?" he asked Pep as they replaced the box of clothing.

"Over this way." Pep nudged the box with his foot.

"I'm getting outa here," Buzzer whispered.

Gus was last out of Tina's house. He shut the inside door, just as it had been, and the screen. Pep and Buzzer were hopping up and down. All three of them disappeared through a hedge at the back of Tina's yard.

They had Thursday to live through before May Day on Friday. The parade was to begin at five o'clock, ending in Hampshire Park at six with a town picnic.

Thursday afternoon they decorated their bikes in Pep's garage. They were riding as outlaws— dressed in black, with red bandannas over their noses and mouths. It was killingly funny to be going as outlaws, knowing what they had done.

"What if that stuff doesn't itch?" Buzzer asked as he wound black crepe paper through his bicycle spokes.

"Marty's friends say it works," replied Gus. "You have to believe!"

"How are they gonna know who did it?" Pep passed the roll of crepe paper to Gus. "We want 'em to know."

"We do?" cried Buzzer.

Gus nodded at him solemnly. "Nanny has to know we don't quit either. And we have *great ideas*—we don't just tell on people all the time. This way she'll know to leave us alone from now on."

"Yeah!" Pep said, pounding his bike seat for emphasis.

A perfect Friday arrived, hot and sunny. School lasted longer than any day Gus could remember. He was so excited he couldn't even draw to calm himself down. For days he'd been dying to ask Marty if the itching powder made people really, really itchy. How did they act? Did they holler or rip off their clothes or what?

Of course he couldn't ask, and he didn't want Buzzer or Pep to know he was worried. So all of those questions kept buzzing in his mind like hornets.

When the bell finally rang, Gus vaulted out of his seat and raced for his locker. He tossed his notebook and math book into his backpack. Across the hall he could hear Nanny, Bethie, and Tina.

"Don't go home!" Tina was saying. "My mom's afraid somebody's gonna be late! We have to go to my house now!"

Gus stuffed his old jean jacket into his backpack. "Come on, Pep. I've got to fix some of our picnic right now. Mom gets home late today."

By a quarter to five, everyone who wanted to march in the May Day Parade was milling around the high school parking lot. Nearly all the grade-school kids had decorated bikes. Small children were pulling wagons loaded with dolls or stuffed animals. Some drove miniature tractors or trucks or fire engines. The grade-school, junior-high, and high-school band kids were tuning up their instruments.

The parade chairman and her helpers were screaming.

"Grade-school band in front! Hurry it up!"

"You little kids, you're next, right here!"

"Sara, stop punching Judy and get that wagon up here! Bobby! Get in line with Kevin!"

Next were special entries. First, a costumed Mexican band made up of high-school Spanish students. Then came eight junior-high kids wearing silvery astronaut outfits. They carried a gigantic spaceship model they'd made in science class. Behind them was a 1950s rock-and-roll band, also composed of older kids. The six-person, green Girl Scout caterpillar wriggled into place after the band.

As the girls went by, holding the caterpillar's sheeted body overhead, Bethie said, "This turtleneck's too small. It's digging at my neck!"

Gus grinned at Pep and Buzzer as they lined up with the decorated bikes just behind special entries. They were the second row of bikes, only a few feet behind the caterpillar.

Then came the junior-high band. "You junior trumpets, get over here this instant if you want to be in the parade!"

The senior Boy Scouts and two Eagle Scouts, flags pointed skyward, moved into place. After them came the high-school cheerleaders in white sweaters and short, navy, pleated skirts. Then the baton twirler, all in white with navy tassels, and last the high-school band. Their uniforms were navy with white braid and white stripes down the legs.

"I am never, *never* doing this again!" Gus heard the parade chairman say as she dashed by on an inspection tour. "I'm about to have a heat stroke and there must be a million kids here! What time is it?"

At the head of the line she jumped up on a chair and yelled some more. "Don't leave your place in line! Keep the parade moving and don't lag behind! And don't drive into people!"

The trumpets trumpeted and the drummers drummed as an answer. The grade-school band leader waved his arms, leading them out of the parking lot and down Parkview to Grove, toward the center of town.

Gus, Pep, and Buzzer rode their outlaws' bikes and watched the caterpillar. It looked good for the first block. Maybe even great, Gus thought, being honest.

When they turned left onto Grove, the boys could hear the caterpillar talking and they biked a little closer.

"I can't wear this shirt!" Bethie was complaining to Nanny, just ahead of her. "It's making me crazy! And these tights are too hot. They're itchy all over."

"Mine, too," Nanny said irritably, "and I have to carry this dumb head, so quit wigglin' around!"

The three outlaws exchanged glances. Pep's eyes shone above his bandanna. "It's working!" he said to Gus.

Ahead of them, the rock-and-roll band began "You Ain't Nothin' But a Hound Dog," and Gus hummed along. " 'And you ain't no friend of mine,' " he sang through his bandanna.

Yes, it was really working and the warm sun helped. He could see the girls scratching their turtlenecks. Every few feet, one of them would tug at the neck of her shirt or itch one leg with the other foot.

"Quit stopping!" Nanny called out. "This

head's gonna tear off if you're not careful!"

"There's something in my shoes," grumbled Tina. "My feet feel all scratchy and funny!"

Buzzer pulled down his bandanna. "Our turn," he said to Gus, who rode in the middle. "Great, huh?"

Gus nodded gleefully as the parade turned left on Center Street for one block. Then they would cut down Springfield to Main so they could march past the judging stand and most of the watching townspeople and parents.

Going down Springfield, the caterpillar got louder.

"I'm taking off these tights!" threatened Kim, the last Girl Scout. "They itch like mad!"

"You better not!" Tina said. "My mom'll have a fit. We have to have green legs!"

"I'm with Kim!" Bethie cried. "I hate these tights!"

"Quit movin' around so much!" Nanny scolded. "This head's gonna come off!"

By now, anyone within fifty feet of the caterpillar knew there was a problem.

"Quit stopping!" bawled the bikers ahead of

Gus's group. Dressed and decorated in red, white, and blue, they each had a large American flag. "We keep bumping into you!"

The caterpillar jerked and hitched its way from one side of the street to the other. By the time the parade turned onto Main Street, there was a long gap between the caterpillar and the rock-and-roll band ahead of them.

The chairman came zipping into view, running along the sidewalk. "What's the matter with you girls? Can't you see that big space ahead of you? Close ranks, close ranks!"

"I keep telling 'em!" Nanny snapped as she relentlessly pulled the caterpillar forward.

The three girls at the end of the caterpillar stopped abruptly and knelt down, making a long bug with its rear on the ground. Only Gus, Pep, and Buzzer knew that the hidden girls were scratching frantically in as much privacy as they could manage. The crowd began to point and laugh.

The chairman ran out into the street. "The whole parade is backed up! Get moving this instant!"

"Come on!" Nanny screeched. "The judges' stand is just one more block!"

The three girls at the rear of the caterpillar raised its body and began walking again in jerky, uneven steps.

The red, white, and blue bikers moved forward, with the outlaws right behind them.

"Hurry up, Nanny!" called Pep. "You're holding up the whole parade!"

"You guys look really weird!" Buzzer called out with unusual bravery. "They look weird, huh, Gus?"

Gus nodded, smiling behind his bandanna. I should be feeling guilty, he thought, but I don't. I'll probably get in a lot of trouble, too, but it's worth it. It's our turn, like Buzzer said.

Just before they got to the judges' stand, Gus said to the red, white, and blue bikers, "Faster! Your flags won't wave if you don't go fast."

The flag bikers speeded up and nearly rammed the caterpillar.

"Look out, you dummies!" squealed Kim, the last Girl Scout. "Nanny, hurry up!"

Nanny whipped around to give the bikers what for, and nearly ripped the head from the body. She had to hold on with two hands and not scratch anywhere. Slowly, awkwardly, the caterpillar jerked its way past the judges' stand.

A few feet past the stand, Kim dropped the sheet and ran for the curb. "I itch so bad I can't stand it! I'm going home!" she called. "This's dumb!"

Bonnie and Diana, the girls ahead of her, dropped their caterpillar portion also. "Me, too!" they cried together.

"We can't pull this thing ourselves!" wailed Tina.

"We have to finish to win!" Nanny screamed.

A few feet later, Bethie stopped too. "I don't care if we win or not," she sobbed. "I itch everywhere and it's all your fault, Nanny. This caterpillar was a dumb idea!"

She ran toward home and Nanny and Tina, crying, hauled the green sheet over to the curb and out of the parade.

Gus, Pep, and Buzzer biked past the dead caterpillar. The perfect crime, Gus thought, watching out of the corner of his eye. Nobody knows anything. Nobody can prove anything.

"I've got a whole bag of marshmallows for roasting at the picnic," he told Pep and Buzzer. "You want some?"

13

The Greatest Idea

No one in Gus's class said much about the May Day Parade after it was over. None had won prizes and they were too busy enjoying the first town picnic of the year. Nanny and her friends arrived late at the picnic. They wore fresh clothes and their hair was wet.

"I bet they had to take showers to get rid of that itching powder," Gus told Pep and Buzzer.

I'll tell her what I did, Gus thought, but not right away. She's too mad now.

He waited through the weekend, deciding

he would tell his mom, too—but not now. He would tell her someday when he was older, when he could explain better why he had had to end the fight with Nanny once and for all.

In school the following week Nanny paid no attention to him and was unusually quiet. She didn't tattle once.

After school on Thursday, Gus walked Figment while he thought of what to say to Nanny. Figment had learned to walk well on a leash, though she preferred chewing it even if it was metal. With proud eyes he watched her bounce down the street. She was the furriest dog he knew, the most loving, and soon she'd be the biggest. Now that she was trained, she slept beside his bed—or on it.

I need to draw her now, while she's still a teenager, he thought. I just wish I could do it better. And Mrs. Davidson can't help.

Still, she had tried. Ever since he had begun working on the art show, Mrs. Davidson had spent extra time with him in class. She had repeatedly said he had talent. But she couldn't teach him to draw animals.

And it's not just animals, he thought. It would be great to draw *everything* and know it was right. So people would say, "Hey, wow! Look at this picture!" Even judges at art contests would say that. There'd be no question about whose was the best, about where the blue ribbon belonged.

The blue ribbon made him think of Nanny again. He couldn't put it off any longer. He ran with Figment back to the house and gave her some dry munchies—a reward for not tugging constantly on the leash. Next he wrote a note for his mother, saying when he would return.

And then he went to Nanny's house. He rang the doorbell, hoping she would answer. Instead it was her mother. "Aren't you Rae Howard's youngest?" Mrs. Vincent asked before he could open his mouth.

"Yes, ma'am. Could Nanny come outside? I need to ask something about our homework."

Mrs. Vincent called for Nanny and left the

doorway. When Nanny saw who was on the steps, she stopped in the entry hall, several feet inside the door. "Go home" was all she said.

This was going to be tougher than he'd figured. He had to get her outside where her mother couldn't overhear.

"I have a big, big secret," he said honestly. "Something you should know. And I'm not kidding."

Nanny tipped her head to one side, her light eyes studying him. Then she said, "Hunh! You lie like a rug."

Gus shrugged. "Okay. Be that way. I can tell Tina . . . or Bethie. I just thought you'd want to know first, that's all." He started to turn away.

"Why Tina or Bethie?" she demanded. Now she was standing closer to the screen.

"I can't tell you if you won't listen. I was just sure you'd want to know first." He inched backward.

Nanny hesitated, then came out onto the steps. Gus moved out into the yard and bent over to snap off a dead flower head in the front garden. He wanted a considerable distance from Mrs. Vincent.

He broke off another dead flower head. She came closer. "Nice flowers," he said.

Nanny's eyes narrowed. "Okay, you've got one minute."

Gus spoke very fast because he didn't want her interrupting—not even once.

"I ruined your caterpillar. I put itching powder in all your clothes and I did it on purpose and I can do it again. I'm sick of this fighting and your telling all the time and every time you tell on me or try to get back at me I'm gonna get back at you worse and I'm never going to give up—never, never! Now are you gonna quit telling or not?"

Nanny flinched at his words. Her eyes got wide and she trembled slightly. When she could talk, it was a whisper. "I thought it was something like that. That's meee-eeen," she said, sounding as if she would burst into tears.

"I know," Gus said, calmer now that he had

told his anger. "Just like *you've* been mean about my accent and telling on me all the time and making fun of me staying after school and showing off about your ribbons."

Nanny seemed riveted in place by his words. Slowly the tears began to trickle down her face and plop onto her shirt.

"And don't go running to your mom, because you can't prove anything. Not a thing! I'll say you're lying because you hate me, and my folks'll believe me. They know you've been tattling all year. So does Mr. Keene."

Nanny's tears came faster. She rubbed at her eyes but the tears didn't stop.

Gus pressed on. "Now is it over? I want it to be over. I hate fighting and telling on people. It stinks."

In spite of himself, Gus was beginning to feel pity. I can't believe it, he thought. I feel sorry for creepy Nanny Vincent. Maybe nobody ever told her off before.

Into his mind flashed a picture of Jut, tapping his head and saying, "Remember?" Jut would want him to use his brain now and forget the anger. He wouldn't like what Gus had done and neither would Marty—or Mr. Keene. Gus sighed. No, it wasn't over yet.

"Look, Nanny, I don't want to fight, but I'm tired of being picked on. Anybody would be, okay?" He moved closer. "I won't pick on you if you don't pick on me. Is it a deal?"

Nanny swallowed noisily and sniffled. "I . . . I won't tell . . . my mom," she said between sobs.

"Okay," he said. He had thought he would run around and shout "Yahoo!" when she knew she was beaten. But he didn't want to do that anymore. That would be gloating. He and Mr. Keene hated gloaters.

"It's . . . a deal," Nanny said. "We're even."

"Okay," he said again. "Good." He started to walk out of her yard, then turned. She was standing right where he'd left her, swiping at her face.

So her mom won't know she's been crying, Gus thought. "Hey?" he called. "Your poster? It was the best. Mrs. Davidson and I knew even before the judges. 'Bye."

That night, after supper, Gus biked to Pep's
house and they went over to Buzzer's. Up in
Buzzer's room, while Grace the collie snored
on the bed, he told them what he had done.
What he had said and what Nanny had said.

"Geez! You didn't have to say her poster
was better than mine!" Pep said.

"Yeah I did." Gus knew Pep couldn't understand, not unless he'd seen Nanny. "Anyway,
it's over now."

"We won!" Pep exulted.

Buzzer shook his head. "We're *even*, like
Nanny said."

The room was quiet then for several seconds.

"So . . ." Pep asked, "what'll we do now?"

"Yeah, what'll we do now?" echoed Buzzer.

Gus grinned. "Do I have to think of everything?"

"Sure!" Pep said. "It's only seven, you know.
I don't have to be in till dark."

What Gus thought of was fishing. They took
poles and canned corn and nightcrawlers out
to the lake at Hampshire Park. Fish liked to

bite in the evenings, they reminded their parents. They would be in by dark.

"Fish love this corn," Pep said, heaving his line out from the end of the boat dock.

"Only the little wimpy ones," Buzzer insisted. "A real fish wants a nightcrawler."

Gus agreed and was threading the fattest nightcrawler in their can onto his hook. He wiped the worm guts onto his jeans and lowered his line next to the dock. Fish often hung around the dock pilings. That's what Marty always said.

It was peaceful fishing at the lake. A mama duck and her teenagers quacked their way sleepily out of the water and up the bank to a grass clump. Out in the middle of the lake, a silvery fish jumped.

"Here, fish, over here," Buzzer called.

Gus and Pep smiled at each other.

"We can do this all summer," said Buzzer. "I wish school was out."

Gus checked his line. The worm was still there and no signs of a nibble. He let it down again, thinking. Do I want to do this all summer?

No, he said silently. Sometimes it'd be okay, but not every day for three months. Super barfo. So what am I going to do? He remembered promising his mother to be good for Marty and Nick, who would be in charge. I could go to camp, maybe, for a couple weeks. Then what?

"Pep, what're you doing this summer?" Gus asked.

"Going to my aunt's farm in Kentucky. I've got tons of cousins there and it's great! I can stay as long as I want. Lucky, huh?"

Buzzer said, "All *my* aunts live in cities and that's pukey, so I just stay home. But this year we can play softball, 'cause we're ten. That'll be great."

"Yeah," Gus said, "I'll play softball, too." Still, that's not enough, he thought.

No fish came to their bait, but as light faded and dark moved in over the lake, an idea came to Gus.

He thought about his idea all the way home and while he kept Figment company for her nightly visit to the yard. What would Buzzer and Pep think? Would they think he was some kind of sissy? A real wimp?

Nah, he decided. The guys said that Pep and I have to win first place next year. It was two girls this year so it's our turn. And our show was lots better than the fifth-graders' show is now. We're the best class in the school! They won't think I'm a wimp.

Figment finished her tour of the yard and came to lie beside him on the porch step, her head in his lap. She bumped his leg with her nose until he began ruffling her furry coat— scratching here, petting there. She whuffed contentedly and enjoyed being loved. They stayed there till the moon rose over the garage.

Gus took her inside. His mind was made up now.

He found his parents in bed, reading and talking with one another. "I've got a question," he said.

Mr. Howard glanced at the clock. "Better be fast, okay? You should be in bed."

165

Gus hopped on the bed. "I am. See?"

His mother put down her book. "Shoot. Only not too tricky, okay? I'm beat."

"It's about summer. Can I take art lessons at the museum? Then I won't give Marty and Nick so much trouble. Isn't that a good idea?"

His dad smiled. "That's a good idea, all right. Have you thought about camp?"

"Yeah. It's okay for a couple weeks. Mom, can I take art lessons? I want to get really good. *Now.*"

"Okay. The museum has wonderful summer classes. But you're sounding rather intense about all this, Gus. You aren't expecting to be a pro after one summer, are you?"

"No, but Mom, I have to get better! Something inside is telling me. I've been listening and it's telling me."

"That's fine, then," she said softly. "I was just about your age when I knew that art was the field for me." She smiled at him. "You'll be extremely good at it, too, if that's what you want."

"Yup. That's what I want," he said, imagining

166

his bedroom wall covered with blue ribbons. "You just wait. This's the greatest idea I ever had."

His dad chuckled. "But not the last, of course?"

"No way!" Gus assured him. "I've got years of good ideas coming. Years!"